Luvvy
and the Girls

"My hair hung down like this when I used to perform on the trapeze," she said. *p. 105*

Luvvy and the Girls

by Natalie Savage Carlson

pictures by Thomas di Grazia

Harper & Row, Publishers

New York, Evanston, San Francisco, London

Also by Natalie Savage Carlson

For the pupils of the
Frederick Academy of the Visitation

Contents

I.

Going Away

The train followed the Potomac River, leaving the rugged Maryland foothills behind. It chugged through gently rolling countryside where corn stood tall in the fields and apple orchards were heavy with rosy-cheeked fruit.

"Going away, going away, going away," the wheels rumbled.

Luvena Savage was going away from the carefree life on the farm, and her childhood. She was twelve years old that early fall day of 1915, and one of the Girls now.

The three girls were going away to boarding-school life with its rules and regulations. They were going away to the Visitation Academy in Frederick where Luvvy, as she was called, had always longed and begged to go.

Hetty and Betsey were her half sisters by Papa's first marriage. But she only thought of them as half sisters when she was angry with them.

Today she felt a deep love and frightened dependence. They had gone away to the convent all their school years, so this was no new experience for them. But how would she fit into this different kind of life? She would have to live with many girls of all ages.

Hetty, almost seventeen years old, sat clutching the big box of candy given her by her new beau. She hadn't even allowed the conductor to put it on the rack above them.

She's pretty now that she's in love, thought Luvvy. She lets her hair curl around her face, and her blue eyes are even bluer. Like the wild chicory flowers I like to pick along the roadside.

Chubby brown-eyed Betsey, three years younger, seemed so different from Hetty. Even now she was slouched on the red plush seat which she had reversed so they could face each other. Her straw hat was askew, and one glove was smudged from trying to raise the window until Hetty cautioned that they might get coal dust over their clothes and cinders in their eyes. Luvvy felt closest to Betsey because she was nearest in age and seemed to get into as much mischief.

"Will you miss having Regina with you this year?" Luvvy asked them.

"Oh, yes," admitted Hetty. "She was really like a mother to us instead of our big sister. Now I'll have to take her place."

As she spoke, she flicked a tiny cinder from her lap. Hetty had always been the Neat One in the family. Luvvy was sure that she would always see to it that they were presentable in appearance.

After graduation Regina had stayed home with Papa and Mama and little Marylou at Shady Grove, their farm. She was waiting to enter the Convent of the Sisters of Charity in Emmitsburg. She wouldn't leave home until after the birth of Mama's new baby in January. Probably she wouldn't leave until the next summer. It really didn't seem right for Regina to go off to be a nursing nun when she was the Beauty of the family.

"Going away, going away, going away," repeated the wheels beneath their coach.

They changed trains at Washington Junction as Mama had so carefully reminded them to do. Since there was a short wait, they went into the depot. There was a big rocking chair near a brass cuspidor, which Luvvy immediately appropriated. Like Mama, she enjoyed rocking. It gave you something to do when sitting down.

"Do you think the other girls will like me?" she asked Betsey. "Will I have a special friend, like you have Mary Leary?"

Mary Leary from Williamsport had visited them that summer. She was a jolly, friendly girl whom Luvvy was especially fond of.

"That will depend on you," said Betsey.

"I never felt that I needed my own friends back home. There were so many of us. But now that I'm older, I hope I have a best friend. Someone to do things with, and share secrets."

They heard the warning whistle of the Frederick train. Luvvy jumped up so suddenly that the chair kept rocking by itself.

The second coach was just like the first, only the seats were covered with green plush instead of red. It was more crowded, so Luvvy shared a seat with an old man reading a newspaper. For awhile she read over his shoulder about the progress of the war in Europe. French troops were digging more trenches in the Champagne region in preparation for an expected breakthrough of the German lines. Europe and the Champagne—so far away from Maryland!

The man turned the page, so she looked out of the window again.

"Look!" she called back to her sisters. "Look at all those horses in the field."

The old man peered over his glasses to look also.

"Race horses," he informed her. "That's the Moore place."

In the field slim-legged horses with proudly-borne heads seemed to flow across the grass instead of walking or trotting. So different from Valley and Dolly, the carriage horses she often rode at Shady Grove.

A large oval track moved past the window, then a stately columned mansion with white picket fences.

"I hear that Mary Letitia Moore is coming to the Academy this year," cried Betsey above the rumble of the wheels. "She and her brother have had governesses up until now. You'll have something in common with her since you're so crazy about horses."

Luvvy was delighted. Any uncertainties about the future vanished. Oh, this life awaiting her was going to be wonderful, delicious, positively enchanting.

"She must be near your age," added Hetty. "But you started with Miss Harriet when you were only five, remember, so some of the girls in your class may be a little older than you."

Luvvy thought of the private tutor in Weverton who had given her so much encouragement in writing her little stories for the children's page of the *Baltimore Sunday Sun*.

But her mind returned to the horses. It had been a

sacrifice to leave them behind. But to be in the same school with a girl whose family owned *race* horses! What wonderful times she and Mary Letitia Moore would have together! Mary Letitia might be her best friend. Perhaps she would even invite Luvvy to visit her. Perhaps, perhaps, impossible, maybe possible, she might even let Luvvy ride one of the race horses. Not to be jounced by Dolly's stiff-legged trot or jolted by Valley's uneven gallop, but to float down a road as if she were riding on a cloud!

"Going away, going away. Frederick town, Frederick town," the wheels chanted. Then as they stopped at small stations and the steam escaped, "Barbara Fritchie, Barbara Fritchie." Frederick was the home of that heroine who had in legend defied Stonewall Jackson's soldiers by waving a Union flag from her window.

Luvvy remembered reciting Whittier's famous poem about her for Miss Harriet.

> *"Shoot, if you must, this old gray head,*
> *But spare your country's flag," she said.*

It had even been on such a day as this.

> *Up from the meadows rich with corn,*
> *Clear in the cool September morn . . .*

It was disillusioning that Papa didn't believe that Dame Fritchie's act of defiance had happened at all.

"Tomfoolery!" Perhaps it was because he was Virginia-born.

But there were "the clustered spires of Frederick" approaching them from the distance. Luvvy had seen them before when she had gone with Papa and Mama in the Machine to visit the Girls at their school. But that had been when she was one of the Children at home. Today Frederick in the distance looked like a town in fairyland. The church spires were towers rising from enchanted castles.

The train slowed, then "Barbara Fritchied" to a stop at the depot. The old man folded his newspaper and stood up. The Girls made their way down the crowded aisle.

"I'll go ahead and see about our trunks and suitcases," said Hetty. "There's a nice baggage man who always looks out for the convent girls' belongings."

Betsey and Luvvy waited beside the tracks.

When Hetty returned she said, "They'll send our things over right away. It's such a nice day, let's save our money by walking."

They sauntered down block after block of brick buildings set close to the brick sidewalk. Luvvy remembered what Papa had said the first time he had driven her through Frederick. "If I had a brick kiln in Frederick instead of a tool factory in Hagerstown, I'd be a millionaire today."

At last they reached old St. John's Church, and

there was the convent across the corner from it. It was an enormous building of brick, with green shutters and a high iron fence in front. It sheltered the Academy and the Monastery, as the nuns' wing was called.

The Girls went up the steps and into the hallway. Hetty straightened Betsey's hat and wiped a smudge off Luvvy's nose with her handkerchief. Then she daintily pushed the inner bell with a white-gloved finger.

"Now I'm here as a pupil," cried Luvvy. "Not just visiting you all with Mama and Papa. This will be my home for another year. Oh, why doesn't Sister Veronica hurry! I can hardly wait for the door to open."

2.

The Little Girls

The little grated window set in the door opened first. It framed the familiar face of Sister Veronica, one of the portresses. She swung the door open, with a broad welcoming smile.

Sister Veronica was an "out nun," as those were called who didn't wear veils and could go out of the convent. In her black cap and capelet, she looked something like the woman who sold eggs near Knoxville.

"How wonderful to have the dear girls back today!" she exclaimed. "It has been such a quiet summer. And how are your dear parents? It's too bad they couldn't bring you—I always enjoy talking with your dear father. He is such a singular gentleman."

"He was too busy to drive us here in the Machine," said Hetty, "so we came by train."

Luvvy burst out, "I've been wanting to come here to school all my life."

She wondered why Sister Veronica laughed as if it were a joke.

"It seems to me that I've been here all my life," the nun explained. "Forty-five years ago last May I entered. Nearly half a century."

Luvvy understood why Sister had laughed at her lifetime of twelve years.

Then Sister Veronica looked sad and serious. "We have been praying daily for the dear little sister you lost," she said.

Luvvy felt sad and serious too. Her eight-year-old sister Maudie, who had been a close companion, had died last summer after being thrown and kicked in the head by a colt. Memory of Maudie was still a sore, bittersweet thing. She didn't want to talk about it—even to Sister Veronica. She was glad when Hetty suggested they go to look for old friends.

Luvvy followed Betsey so closely that she stepped on her heel twice as they walked down a long hall whose floor was shiny and slippery with varnish. She was in alien territory now, and she felt a need for protection until she became familiar with it.

A group of chattering girls were gathered around

a nun near an open door. The nun broke away to greet the newest arrivals.

"The Savage girls!" she exclaimed. "It's so nice to have you back again. And with your little sister. But we'll miss Regina."

Hetty and Betsey affectionately touched cheeks with the nun.

"You remember Luvvy," said Hetty. "She's been here before with Papa and Mama Della. Luvvy, you remember Sister Mary Cecilia who taught me last year."

The nun's starched white barbette crackled as she leaned over to proffer her cool cheek to Luvvy.

She said to her, "The Big Girls will want to look for their old friends, so I'll take you to meet some of the Little Girls who will be in your grade."

"I'll be in the eighth grade," said Luvvy quickly. It was discouraging to learn that here at the convent instead of the Girls and the Children, they had the Big Girls and the Little Girls. Would she have to wait another year to be one of the Big Girls? Up to now, she had been one of the Children at home.

Luvvy regretfully let Sister Mary Cecilia lead her to an outside door.

"I'll take you to Amy Ackroyd," said the nun. "I just saw her on the porch. You'll love Amy. She is an angel—one of our sweetest girls."

Luvvy saw that she would have strong competition

11

for the gold medal for deportment, which she had hoped to win ever since she had seen Hetty's.

She wished she could stay with Betsey. She really wasn't ready to meet strange girls yet. Maybe they wouldn't even like her. Her hand grew hot and moist as she clung to Sister Mary Cecilia's cool one.

The nun led her out on a porch that overlooked the convent grounds. A high white brick wall and more buildings shut off two sides of the grounds. The feeling of being closed in was a new one for Luvvy, who had wandered open fields and followed inviting paths with complete freedom. But it did seem peaceful and cozy here.

Tensely she looked at two girls standing near the railing. One had long blond curls, big blue eyes, and the face of an angel. The other was the exact opposite—a thin, homely little girl with stringy brown hair and a pinched face.

"Girls," Sister Mary Cecilia commanded their attention, "I want you to meet one of our new girls, little Luvena Savage. Luvena, this is Amy Ackroyd and here, Agatha Mulcahy. Amy, I want you to take special care of Luvena. I must return to the Big Girls."

As Sister Mary Cecilia swept away, Luvvy felt completely deserted. She was tongue-tied with shyness. What should she say to these strange girls? Probably the same thing she always said to adults

when she met them for the first time.

"It's so nice to meet you," she said stiffly.

The girls studied her as closely as she studied them. The angel was the first to speak.

"It's even nicer to have you here, Luvena," she said. "I know you'll love the Academy. The nuns are so sweet."

"I've been eager to come here with my older sisters," answered Luvvy. "But please call me Luvvy. Everyone at home does." That sounded friendly, didn't it?

"I'll try," offered Amy. "The nuns don't like nicknames, but I want you to be happy. Don't you love to make people happy?"

Luvvy was guilt-ridden. Most of the things she did were to make herself happy. Amy was truly an angel. She would try to be like her. It would be so much easier if she could have golden curls and an angel face instead of straight black braids and a coppery tan.

"It may seem lonely at first," said Agatha. "I cried and cried when I first came. That was probably because my mother and father had just died. But Sister Veronica is my great-aunt so I really have someone close to me here."

"And since I have two older sisters," said Luvvy, "I'm with part of my family."

After this information, she fell silent again. What should she talk about now? Amy solved the problem.

"Where is your home?" she asked.

"We live on a farm on the Potomac," said Luvvy. "Near Weverton, but I'm sure you never heard of it. It's so small. Where do you come from?"

She wished her voice didn't sound so artificial. As if she were reciting a piece.

"My father has a plantation on the eastern shore," said Amy, "but we live in Baltimore. It's such a big city that there's a lot to see and do."

Luvvy was more impressed by the plantation than by Baltimore. No one in western Maryland ever called a farm a plantation, no matter how vast its acreage.

There was a lull in the conversation while Luvvy tried to think of something else to say.

"There's Auntie Sister beckoning to me now," explained Agatha, "so I must go. 'Bye, Luvvy. See you in chapel, Amy." She hurried away.

"Do we have to go to chapel this afternoon?" asked Luvvy. She knew they would have to attend Mass every morning because that was why she had the black veil for weekdays and the white one for Sundays. But she didn't think they'd be rushed into chapel on the very afternoon of their arrival.

Amy made a cute little face.

"That's just a joke with Agatha," she explained. "But I think it's irreverent, don't you? Come on down the steps and let's walk in the yard together so we can get acquainted."

Such a kind, friendly girl, this Amy Ackroyd. Luvvy felt flattered yet humble. She would like to have her for a best friend, if possible.

Their high-laced shoes crunched over the dirt paths that wound between great elms and maples whose trunks were circled by rustic benches.

"Is Agatha Mulcahy your best friend?" asked Luvvy. She felt a prick of jealousy.

"Oh, no," said Amy, "but I try to be specially nice to Agatha because she's a poor girl. She's a charity student, you know."

"She seems like a real nice girl," said Luvvy.

"That's why I feel so sorry for her," continued Amy. "I'm so happy that she can fit into the dresses I outgrow. That's one of mine she's wearing today."

Luvvy decided to change the subject by asking about the girl who couldn't be accused of poverty.

"Has the other new girl, Mary Letitia Moore, come yet?" she asked.

"I heard she won't be here for a few weeks," answered Amy, "because she went on a trip to California with her parents this summer. She's real rich, so I hope she won't be stuck-up. Even if my papa was a millionaire, I wouldn't be stuck-up. Would you? I'd help poor orphans like Agatha all I could."

Luvvy wasn't sure how a million dollars would

16

affect her, since Papa didn't have a brick kiln in Frederick.

They reached the playground in front of the garden shrine where some Very Little Girls were playing hopping games, then they turned back.

"Let's sit down on a bench for awhile," suggested Amy.

They did so and leaned back against the rough elm trunk. Luvvy had a good view of the Academy buildings. They rose four stories high, porch upon porch, over arcaded walkways.

"What a wonderful place to commit suicide!" she exclaimed. "Somebody could jump off that highest porch."

Amy was shocked. "It's a mortal sin to do that. How can you even think of such a thing?"

"I didn't mean to do it myself," explained Luvvy. "I was just thinking of a story I could write. I'm going to be a writer when I grow up." That should impress Amy.

But the other girl's sweet face was filled with disapproval. "I don't think you should even write about such things. It's sinful."

Luvvy was beginning to feel uncomfortable. Perhaps it was because she wasn't used to girls her own age. Would she ever feel at ease with them?

She had an overwhelming desire to flee to the protection of Betsey.

"It's been nice talking to you," she suddenly said, "but I've got to get back to my sisters. They may be looking for me."

She knew she was being rude, but the urge to get away was too strong.

Amy had a hurt look on her angelic face. "Of course, Luvvy, if you don't want to talk to me any-more."

"It—it isn't that. I have to go," said Luvvy desperately.

For the rest of the time, she stayed close to Betsey. She was glad that Mary Leary was with her instead of some strange girl.

They stood on a lower porch and watched trunks being raised to the attic. Long ropes hung down four stories. The workmen bound each trunk. Then a man on the highest porch turned a crank and the trunk slowly ascended, to the cheers of the girls below.

"They say a girl went up with her trunk, for a lark, once," said Betsey.

"She must have had to sit on the penance bench for a month," said Mary.

Sitting in silence on a hard bench for a specified time was the usual punishment for misdemeanors.

"Where are the penance benches?" asked Luvvy.

Mary pointed to two pewlike benches against a wall of the arcaded brick walk. "Those are the out-side ones, and there are more in the playroom. Of

18

course you can sit on them any time you want. They aren't just for punishment."

Agatha, who was near the pile of trunks below, waved—but Luvvy pretended not to see her. No one was going to separate her from Betsey.

Only supper in the refectory could do that. When the girls trooped into the big room with its wooden pillars and rows and rows of tables, Luvvy found herself back with the Little Girls.

Each table accommodated eight girls. There was an empty place awaiting Mary Letitia Moore. Although Luvvy was separated from familiar faces, she was happy to recognize her own napkin ring that had been brought from home.

She found herself between Amy and a red-haired, freckle-faced girl who turned out to be Mabel Courtney.

They said grace, then sat down. Great silver urns were carried to the table by the domestic nuns, who wore white veils. An urn was set at the head of each table, and the girl there ladled out a thick soup. Hot biscuits, as puffy and white inside as snowballs, were passed around. And there was a drink that was more milk than tea.

Luvvy spooned her soup and listened to the conversation that skipped around her. The girls chattered and giggled about the things that had happened the year before.

"I wanted to take harp lessons this year," said Eunice Somebody, a very pretty girl who looked like a china doll with her big staring eyes and short taffy-colored curls. "Didn't the two Big Girls who played the harps on the stage at Commencement look beautiful? But Mama says I have to keep on with piano."

"I'm going to take harp when I get in high school next year," said Amy. "Mama thinks I should be more mature for it." She threw a conversational bait to Luvvy. "Do you play anything, Luvvy?"

Luvvy answered apologetically, "Miss Marmion used to come from Harpers Ferry to teach me piano, but I never could learn to play a piece all the way through without hitting a lot of wrong notes. Papa let me quit because he said I played the scales well enough."

Agatha nodded. "I wouldn't even know if a piano was in tune."

Amy looked disappointed with them. "I think anyone with beautiful thoughts would want to express them in music, don't you?"

Luvvy was silent for the rest of the meal. She had tried to think of how to bring horses into the conversation, but they didn't seem to fit in with pianos and harps. If only Mary Letitia were here at the table! She surely wouldn't act stuck-up when she found out that Luvvy was interested in horses too.

After supper the girls went to the playroom, a

spacious room equipped with chairs and tables. A nun sat at one table to keep an eye on them.

Luvvy immediately returned to Betsey's side. She and Mary Leary were playing double solitaire with a worn deck of cards. Hetty was at another table with her own friends.

"Maybe you'd like to ask some of the Little Girls to play with us," suggested Mary. "We can play Old Maid."

"I don't know them well enough yet," answered Luvvy. "I'd rather play with just you all. I'll deal, if you want."

But she was separated from them again by the night bell. Those who needed to went to the "jacks," the outhouse at the end of the arcade.

Finally, the girls lined up for prayers, according to height, with the Very Little Girls tapering off at the end. Although Luvvy was slightly younger than Agatha Mulcahy, she was taller, so she stood just ahead of her in line. They knelt on the hard floor and responded to prayers led by the nun.

They turned and started the long walk to the dormitory on the third floor. Despite the tramp of so many feet up the bare stairs and through long dark rooms, Luvvy felt lonely. What were they doing at home now? They surely weren't going to bed so early. Only Marylou anyway.

Each girl turned into her little cubicle and pulled

21

the white curtains shut to be alone with her brass bed, washstand, and clothes tree.

Luvvy was pleased that Betsey's "curtain," as each cubicle was called, was across the aisle and not far down the row from hers. They could slip back and forth quite easily.

Betsey, in long flannel nightgown, soon joined her younger sister for a few minutes' chat before sleep.

"How do you like the convent?" she asked.

Luvvy slowly poured water from the pitcher into her bowl. Her voice was as forced as it had been in making conversation with Amy.

"It's real nice," she said.

But there was a lump in her throat. She wanted to cry. She wanted to get on the train and go home. She wanted to be back at Shady Grove with Mama and Papa and Regina and Marylou. What crazy notion made children want to grow up and get away from home?

3.
History and Politics

Luvvy was awakened by the clanging of a bell. In the first fuzzy moments she thought it was the farm bell calling the men in from the fields.

Her eyes opened to whiteness. She was surrounded by white curtains. One of them jerked open.

"Wake up, Luvvy!" ordered Betsey. "Time for Mass. We have only fifteen minutes to get ready."

Luvvy came fully awake. She leaped out of bed and went to the clothes tree. She buttoned her undervest on and kicked into her black sateen bloomers. Then the cotton underskirt. She poured water into the bowl, splashing some on the wooden floor, and gave her face a quick birdbath. Then the new navy-blue dress. Finally the black sateen apron which was the badge of the Little Girls. The Big Girls didn't wear aprons.

She hurried, proud to be a boarding-school girl and adaptable to such rules. Gone was the homesickness of the night before. Homesickness can't thrive in early morning activity. She was thrilled and happy again. How wonderful to be at the convent with the Girls!

Luvvy took the black veil from the washstand drawer and draped it over her head and shoulders.

She bumped into Betsey in the aisle.

"Oh, pshaw!" exclaimed Betsey. "I forgot to bring my veils down from the trunk. Now I'll have to climb all the way up to the attic during play period, and I'll get a demerit too."

The girls had to go into chapel with covered heads.

She took her handkerchief from her pocket and fastened it precariously to her hair. Betsey had once caused a scandal. At the sound of the chapel bell, she had come running from the jacks with a piece of toilet paper pinned to her hair, and had gotten *three* de-merits.

Again Luvvy found herself with the Little Girls in a pew near the front. She looked over the heads of the wriggly Very Little Girls. She didn't feel very devout. She kept thinking about her new life and the family at home. She thought about Mary Letitia Moore and hoped she wouldn't be stuck-up. The priest's Latin words were a mumble in the background of her thoughts.

There were more bells and breakfast before the eighth-graders gathered in Sister Mary Clare's schoolroom. They were augmented by the day pupils who came in from town. Luvvy was apprehensive when she saw that her desk was paired with Amy's. She hoped Amy wasn't mad because of her abrupt departure the day before. But the other girl smiled sweetly.

Sister began the class by telling the girls the history of Frederick Visitation Convent.

"Would you believe that our spacious buildings began with a log cabin built before the Revolution?" she asked.

All the girls believed it because they had heard the story before. Luvvy was sure the information was for her.

"It was in 1824 that five Sisters of Charity moved into the cabin and started a school."

Luvvy drank in the words. Why hadn't her oldest sister Regina told her that the Sisters of Charity had been here first?

"But they weren't able to continue with it because they had so many hospitals, orphanages, and missions to staff. So our order took it over in 1846. By that time it was a handsome, two-story building."

Luvvy wondered what had happened to the cabin.

Was it the little bake house on the other side of the yard where the bread was still baked in old brick ovens?

"Then the Civil War came close to Frederick. The convent was turned into a hospital for the soldiers wounded at Antietam and Monocacy. Sisters of Charity came back to nurse them. Because of the nearby fighting, some of the girls weren't able to go home. They were moved into the monastery side with the nuns. Sister Mary Martha was a young novice then, so she has many interesting stories to tell."

Luvvy remembered having seen an aged nun shuffling through the garden.

How terrible to be marooned here during a big war! She would worry about the family on the Potomac. She would want to share danger with them. They surely would have been in danger because Sam, the hired man, had turned up two cannonballs in the cornfield when he was plowing. Old Mr. Johnson in Harpers Ferry had fought on the Union side. To think that Sister Mary Martha was something of a Civil War veteran herself!

And why hadn't Regina told her that the Sisters of Charity had nursed the wounded? Maybe that was why she had decided to become a Sister of Charity instead of a Visitandine, as the Visitation nuns were called.

"This very room was the operating room," continued Sister Mary Clare, "and the music room was the ward for the wounded after the battle of Antietam."

Luvvy looked around at the classroom with its grouped desks and blackboards. She imagined Sister Mary Clare's desk as an operating table. A wounded Confederate soldier groaned on it as Regina, winged white cornet on head, bent over him with a pad of chloroform.

She envisioned Regina straightening with shock as she cried, "Alec!" The handsome soldier was Alec Garrett, to whom she had been engaged before she had decided to enter the convent. But in Luvvy's vision, it was too late for them. Regina had become a nun and Alec was dying a hero. As in the novel by F. Marion Crawford the girls had read that summer, *The White Sister*.

The rest of the morning was quite routine with Sister Mary Clare, assisted by Amy, passing out books, pencils, pens, and tablets. In this classroom they would study arithmetic, spelling, geography, history, composition and rhetoric, and penmanship.

Sister wrote some assignments on the blackboard with sweeping gestures. She had beautiful white hands—like white doves fluttering, thought Luvvy. She would use that expression in a story sometime.

Luvvy was sure that Sister Mary Clare knew that her hands were beautiful. She had often wondered what sins women as holy as nuns could ever find to confess weekly. Now she could almost hear Sister whispering through the grating, "And I have been vain about my hands daily."

She dropped her eyes to her desktop in shame. Luvvy felt as guilty as if she had actually eaves-dropped at the confessional.

Finally the big bell rang for midday dinner. Luvvy suddenly realized that she was very hungry.

The girls formed lines and clattered down the steps to the refectory. The warm fragrant smells coming from the kitchen sharpened their appetites. Amy said a quick grace for their table, then chairs scraped as they seated themselves. The domestic nun carried in one big urn after another.

The conversation was mostly about what they had done that summer.

"Of course I stayed here at the convent," said Agatha, "but the nuns tried to make it interesting. They played games with me, and Auntie Sister and Sister Mary Rose sometimes took me for walks to the Jug Bridge outside town." She turned to Luvvy. "They call it that because there's a big brick jug on one end. We picked wildflowers on the way and put them in vases for the shrines when we got back."

Luvvy didn't think that was very interesting.

"I saw some plays in town," said Amy. "But the most fun was when we went to the plantation for two

weeks. Mama had garden parties and I collected butterflies. I caught the most beautiful Tiger Swallowtail
with my net. But my kitten ruined them all before I
could mount them."

"What did you do?" Agatha asked Luvvy.

Luvvy shrugged her shoulders. She didn't want to
tell them. There had been so many sad things that
she didn't want to talk about. Maudie's death after
the colt had kicked her in the head. The time that
Pepper, her favorite horse, had been struck by a train.
And Sam, the hired man she liked so much, had been
discharged because of his drinking.

"I rode horseback a lot," she said in a disinterested
voice.

"We have a Kentucky Thoroughbred on the plantation," put in Amy, "though Mama is the only one
who rides. But this summer she spent a lot of time
helping Papa. He's going to run for the state legisla-
ture, you know."

"My father will vote for him if he's a Democrat,"
said Mabel.

"My father is a Democrat too," added Eunice.

"And mine," echoed the other girls.

"Papa is a *Jeffersonian* Democrat," said Amy im-
portantly.

Luvvy felt the need to support her father's party.

"My father is a Republican and so am I," she announced. "He says that when he lived in Virginia

he was probably the only Republican in the state."

The girls looked at her with shock and distaste.

"Then he must not have voted for President Wilson," said Eunice reproachfully.

"We were for Taft," said Luvvy.

The air grew chillier.

"I don't see how anyone could be a Republican," said Amy. "It's so—so unreasonable."

Luvvy flushed. She was beginning to feel as if she were in a state of mortal sin.

"But I like President Wilson," she confessed, "and I've even seen him in person."

"Really!" exclaimed Agatha. "In Washington?"

"No. He rode right past our house with Mrs. Galt. They were on their way to have lunch at the Hilltop House in Harpers Ferry. There were two other cars, with Secret Service agents in them. One drove in front and the other in back of his."

The girls were vitally interested.

"What does Mrs. Galt look like?" asked Eunice. "Is she as pretty as they say?"

"I guess so," said Luvvy, "because she looks a lot like Mama. She's a brunette and she wore such a stylish hat. She was sitting down so I don't know if she's stout like Mama or not. And the President wears glasses and has a lot of teeth when he smiles. I saw him smile at her. I hope they'll get married."

They seemed to have forgiven her for being a Republican. Perhaps she was lucky. She remembered that when Hetty had been a Little Girl during an election year, some of the Big Girls pushed her into a corner and pinched her until she promised to be for William Jennings Bryan instead of Taft.

Mabel said, "I just don't think it's fair that a Republican should see him when we didn't." They looked at Luvvy as if she had done something dishonest.

Luvvy fell silent. She finished eating her hash and vegetables. She had never before liked meat and potatoes mixed together, but this convent hash was delicious—the meat all ground up and the potatoes finely chopped.

She looked longingly at the table where Betsey sat. The girls there were talking and laughing so gayly. She was sure they weren't talking about politics. Would she get to sit at Betsey's table when she became a Big Girl? A long, long year away.

After supper that evening it was still light, so the girls went outside again for recreation. A group of Little Girls were playing baseball with a tennis racket.

Luvvy sat with Betsey on a bench. She looked across the patterned plots of grass. Two gray birds trimmed in white were fluttering around the hedge that divided the nuns' recreation grounds from those of the girls.

"What kind of birds are those, Luvvy?" asked Betsey.

Luvvy was the authority on nature because she was so interested in birds and animals.

"Mockingbirds," she said. "They probably have a nest in the hedge. They imitate the songs of other birds, so that's why they're called mockingbirds."

She began whistling to them.

"Don't whistle," warned Betsey. "It's against the rules."

For a few moments Luvvy gazed dreamily at the birds.

"If I were in their place, I wouldn't build a nest here," she said. "I'd fly over the walls and cornfields and woods all the way to the Potomac. I'd build a nest in our aspen tree, then I could watch Papa and Mama and the others all day long."

Without warning she raised her black apron to her face and began to cry.

"What's wrong?" asked Betsey in alarm.

"I wish I were a bird," sobbed Luvvy. "I'd fly straight home."

Betsey put her arm around Luvvy and tried to comfort her.

"You're just homesick," she said. "If you'd make friends with the other girls, you'd get over it."

"I want to be with my own family. I don't think the girls even like me."

Two of them who were playing backfield in the ball game came running over.

"What's wrong with Luvvy?" asked Agatha.

"She twisted her ankle a little," said Betsey, "but it's all right now. Isn't it, Luvvy?"

Luvvy nodded as she dried her eyes on her apron. "It's all right," she assured them.

"That's good," said Eunice. "Why don't you come and play with us? But if your ankle hurts—"

Betsey gave Luvvy a push. "It doesn't hurt her anymore. She was just wishing she could play with you. Go along with them, Luvvy."

4.

Cones, Candy, and Pickles

The girls looked forward to Saturday. Especially Luvvy. By the end of the week the convent walls seemed closing in on her. She wanted to get out on the city streets and see adults—*real* people who weren't nuns—and cars driving around and horses pulling carts and busy shops.

It was a relief to take off the juvenile apron for the afternoon. The dye in the black sateen did have a queer, unpleasant smell—like singed chicken feathers. Then she put on the new blue suit with its high waist and longer skirt. She caressed her purse with the bright nickel inside.

Again she was exasperated at being a Little Girl.

They could spend only a nickel in town, but the Big Girls were allowed a dime from their allowances. Lucky Big Girls! Next year, she would have a whole dime to spend. If she returned next year.

Each Saturday the important decision was how to spend the money. A nickel would buy a bag of candy at the Misses Beckley's shop or an ice cream cone at Dutrow's confectionary or two big, sour pickles at Zimmerman's. Of course there were the luscious meringues at Dutrow's—great balls of ice cream inside a meringue shell—but they cost a quarter, so no one could afford them until Commencement Week, when they could spend all the money left in their yearly allowances.

"I don't know whether to buy a cone or operas," said Luvvy.

Operas were a delicious kind of taffy that no one in the world but the Beckleys knew how to make. It was said that they had been offered big sums of money for their recipe, but refused to reveal the secret.

"I'm going to buy pickles and a cone," said Betsey. "Since you only have a nickel to spend, Luvvy, I'll give you a bite of my pickles."

"And I'll share my candy with you," offered Hetty. "Maybe I'll buy a cone too." She opened her handbag and looked at the shiny dime. "But why don't I buy the cones for Luvvy and me? You, Betsey, buy the pickles and operas. And we'll share them."

"But I don't want to divide two pickles among three people," said Betsey. "I want all of one for myself. And what about my ice cream cone?"

"I'm all mixed up now," said Hetty. "Let's see. My dime will buy the cones and yours the pickles and operas. And we can use Luvvy's nickel for operas too, so we'll have lots of candy to take back."

The girls walked two abreast in a long procession with Sister Mary Rose at the head, and Sister Veronica bringing up the rear with the Very Littlest Girl clinging to her hand.

By the time they reached Dutrow's, Luvvy decided to buy her own ice cream cone.

"That will leave fifteen cents between Betsey and me after I pay for mine," Hetty reckoned, "so we'll buy five cents worth of pickles and ten cents worth of operas to divide. You can have a whole pickle, Betsey, and give the other to Luvvy. And if you help buy the operas, Luvvy and I will give you the cone parts and just eat the ice cream from them. They really taste as good, you know."

They ate their cones inside the confectionary shop because eating was not allowed on the street. It was a very unladylike practice.

Luvvy ate slowly to savor each taste of the cold sweet ball. Because she was so slow, milky trickles ran down the side and Betsey complained, "You're getting my cone all soggy." So Luvvy licked upward,

sculpturing the ice cream into a snowy peak, enjoy-
ing the icy touch to her tongue and the creamy film
left on her lips.

She wondered if all these gallons of ice cream had
been turned by hand as they did it in the home freezer,
with Mama sprinkling salt on the ice from time to
time.

Hetty finished hers first and handed the empty cone
to Betsey. She always managed to keep hers neat and
dry.

Betsey had just bitten into it when Sister Veronica
came hurrying to her.

"Dear child, don't eat that," she admonished. "A
dear lady told me only the other day that the cone is
very indigestible and ruinous to the complexion." She
clapped her hands for attention. "Throw away your
cones, girls, when you finish the ice cream. They are
bad for your health."

"But I like it," protested Betsey. "It's just some
kind of cookie." She bit off a big piece.

"No, no!" forbade Sister Veronica. "We wouldn't
want you to get sick. Your dear parents would never
forgive me. Throw it away."

Betsey cracked off another bite then ruefully threw
the cone into a nearby trashcan. Luvvy's soggy one
soon followed.

"I should get both pickles," Betsey declared.

"But I'm supposed to get some of the pickles too,"

put in Luvvy. "And I wouldn't have had the cone if I knew all I'd get was the ice cream."

They were still arguing about it when the nuns herded them into Zimmerman's.

The old German proprietor fished out two crisp, warty pickles from a barrel that was the same shape as he was. He let them drip a few seconds. Then he dropped them into a paper sack and handed it to Betsey.

The candy shop was the most popular stop. The girls crowded into it. Those in front were pressed against the glass cases.

Such difficult decisions to make. Chocolates that were tiny treasure chests filled with nuts, raisins, and marshmallow. Fiery cinnamon drops—burning coals of spice and sugar. Snappy licorice whips and peppermint sticks like Lilliputian barber poles. And the operas, in twists of wax paper, were shiny translucent bows. Oh, the glorious taste and smell and sight of it all after a week of vegetables and boiled meat and pudding desserts!

"We made a mistake somewhere," said Hetty looking into her handbag. "I thought we were going to have two nickels for operas."

"I handed you my nickel when Mr. Zimmerman gave me back my change," said Betsey.

"You must have forgotten to. It isn't here."

"But I did."

"Then I must have lost it. We can get only one nickel's worth of operas for all of us."

Betsey fell into deep thought for a few minutes. She finally announced, "If I divide my pickles with Luvvy, I'll only have two and a half cents worth of pickles. And after we divide the candy evenly, I'll only have one and two-thirds cents of operas. So all I get is four and one-sixth cents worth of the goodies."

Arithmetic was Betsey's best subject. She had been busy figuring this out in her head.

"We lost your nickel," explained Hetty.

"But since we're spending twenty cents, I should get six and two-thirds cents worth to be even with you all."

"We'll figure it out when we get back to the convent," said Hetty.

"I don't need to get back to the convent to figure out I'm being cheated," protested Betsey.

The younger Miss Beckley came to wait on them. Binnie Beckley was so fat that only the bow on the back of her apron showed where her waist should be. Luvvy supposed that she sampled every batch of candy as it came from the stove in the back kitchen.

When all the purchases had been made, the girls walked back to the convent. Most of them clutched little bags of candy.

Two boys playing on a fence across the street began

to chant, "Convent girls, convent girls, lace drawers and false curls."

The girls haughtily tilted their noses, and the nuns increased the tempo of the march.

As they filed past one of the big brick houses near the convent, an old lady sitting on the porch began frantically gesticulating to Sister Veronica. She was pointing at someone in the line. Sister hurried up ahead.

"Stop the line, Sister," she called to Sister Mary Rose. The girls stopped and stared. What had somebody done now? Luvvy wondered if the lost nickel had been found.

Sister Veronica went to Betsey.

"What is that in your cheek, Elizabeth?" she demanded.

"Which cheek, Sister?" lisped Betsey out of the right corner of her mouth.

"Your *left* cheek," said Sister Veronica. "You surely haven't developed mumps."

Betsey quickly swallowed and her eyes watered. "It was a piece of pickle, Sister."

The old lady on the porch nodded vigorously. "I saw her eating something," she tattled, "so I thought you should know, Sister."

"One of the nuns' spies," mumbled Mabel Courtney, who was Luvvy's partner.

"Thank you, Mrs. Wilkins," said Sister Veronica. "I regret that you had to witness such a vulgar sight. When we get back to the convent, Elizabeth, you will sit on the penance bench for fifteen minutes."

Betsey looked sullen. The long line snaked across the street toward the iron gate of the convent entrance.

Betsey tried to argue with Sister Veronica over her punishment. "I think fifteen minutes is too long for just a bite of pickle," she argued. "I only had it in my mouth for about six seconds."

Sister Veronica turned to the nearby girls.

"Will anyone volunteer to take Elizabeth's punishment for her?" she asked.

It was a common practice to make this request if there was any complaint about the punishment. Having another take her punishment gave the culprit a double sense of guilt.

Mary Leary and two other girls raised their hands.

"I'll take my own punishment," declared Betsey. She stomped to the nearest bench.

Luvvy felt sorry for Betsey.

"I'm going to give her my share of the candy and pickle," she told Hetty. "After all, I had ice cream."

Hetty felt sorry for Betsey, too, so she gave up her share of the operas although she was sure that Betsey had never given her the nickel.

So after serving her sentence on the bench, Betsey

feasted on pickles and most of the candy. She generously gave her sisters some of the operas.

"Let's make it simple next Saturday," suggested Hetty. "Let's put all our money together and buy a meringue. We can have it sliced into three pieces and eat it there."

Later Betsey had a bad pain in her stomach and had to go to the infirmary for medicine.

"You see, my dear," said Sister Veronica triumphantly, "it is the cone you were eating. That proves they are bad for the health."

"It wasn't the cone, Sister," retorted Betsey. "I know it was that big bite of pickle I had to swallow whole."

Luvvy confidentially told Hetty, "I'm sure it was all the pickles and most of our operas she ate."

That night as they undressed for bed and Hetty pulled off her dress, something clinked on the floor and rolled under the bed. It was Betsey's nickel. Then she remembered that she had absentmindedly dropped it into her pocket instead of her handbag.

"Oh, well," said Luvvy cheerfully when Betsey relayed the news to her, "tomorrow is Sunday, and maybe Mama and Papa will come to visit us."

"We haven't been here long yet," said Betsey. "I don't think they'll come so soon."

Luvvy felt that if they didn't come next day she would die of unhappiness. If only she could work up the nerve to ask them to take her home with them. At home they could eat all the pickles they wanted. There were jars and jars of them on the shelves in the cellar. No one ever stopped with one scoop of ice cream. They never had to compute fractions worth of candy because Regina made pans and pans of fudge or penuche at one time. And when they went into Brunswick, they always ate the crusty cones and none of them had a bad complexion. If Mama and Papa came tomorrow, she would hint that she wanted to go home. At most, she might wait until Christmas vacation.

But that was ages and ages away. It was still summery weather.

5.

"The Vengeance of the Sword"

Sunday, beginning with Mass at St. John's Church across the street, was a long, long day. But it had the chance of being the most exciting day of the week. It was on Sunday that the family drove to Frederick to visit the Girls. Not every Sunday. That was the chance of it. If the weather was good and Papa wasn't too tired and Mama was in good health and the Machine was in running order. Even under these conditions, they didn't come every Sunday because it was a long drive with some stretches of road only fit for a horse and buggy.

On quiet Sundays the chimes from St. John's Church sounded louder than on weekdays. In the morning they sounded encouraging. Ding, dong, ding, dong. It's nearly noon. Come soon, come soon. The family could be expected to arrive any time after noon.

Luvvy felt the chimes couldn't ring often enough to bring the afternoon. Why did time have to go so slowly when you were in a hurry for something?

Some of the girls were studying for Monday classes. Others were walking arm in arm on the garden paths, but no one had invited her to join. She would feel silly walking around all by herself.

Betsey had her nose in a book. Hetty was writing a letter—to Alec, of course. He had been engaged to Regina before she decided to become a nun, but he was her beau now. Luvvy sat on an outside penance bench swinging her feet. It gave her a feeling of nonchalance to sit on the bench when she didn't have to.

The Little Girls had split up into groups, some just chatting and others playing quiet games.

Suddenly something drew them into one big group. They started toward the porch steps. Catching sight of Luvvy by herself, Agatha called, "Want to play hide-and-seek with us?"

Luvvy's face brightened. That would help pass the time. And she had often thought of how many nooks there were for hiding on the grounds. Behind a tree, especially the twin elms. In the bushes by the shrine of Our Lady of the Way. Behind the outside stairs.

But the girls were headed for the playroom door.

"Aren't we going to play out here?" asked Luvvy.

"It's more fun in the playroom," replied Agatha.

But where would they hide in the playroom? The tables and chairs and thin posts and potted palms were no good.

She followed them with disappointment.

"It's your turn to be it," Mabel said to Eunice. "Last time we played, the night bell rang."

"Count to a hundred this time," said Agatha. "You never give us time enough."

Eunice braced her forehead against a post and began to count, "One, five, ten, fifteen, twenty, thirty—"

Luvvy desperately looked around for a suitable hiding place. Agatha grabbed her hand. "Come! This way!"

The girls all scurried for the coatroom at the other end of the room. They squeezed into it. Agatha pulled the door shut and bolted it just in time.

"A hundred and one and a half," cried Eunice. "I'm coming."

The girls were frantically grabbing coats and sweaters from the hooks.

"Here, Luvvy," cried Agatha excitedly. "Put this coat over your head. I hear her coming."

Each girl covered her head with an article of clothing. They squealed and giggled.

"She's pulling the chair to the transom," warned

Mabel. "Everybody get down." She peeped through the sleeve of her coat. "She's looking through the transom now."

The girls crouched lower.

"That's Amy under the red sweater," came Eunice's voice through the transom glass.

The girls giggled and made no move.

Eunice continued making guesses, none of which was right. Luvvy was perspiring from the heat generated by so many crowded bodies. The close air was full of the smell of singed chicken feathers. Perhaps the family had already arrived, and here she was squatting in a coat closet. She felt as if she would suffocate if something didn't happen. She pulled the coat off her head to get a breath of air.

"Luvvy," cried Eunice triumphantly. "I see Luvvy with the plaid coat."

The door burst open and the girls erupted, giggling and chattering.

"Luvvy's it. You're it now, Luvvy, and don't count like Eunice did. That wasn't fair."

They escorted her to the far post and a new game began.

"One, two, three, four," counted Luvvy. She was so bored with the whole thing that she counted slowly.

When she turned, the playroom was empty except for a few Big Girls studying at the tables, and a group of Very Little Girls playing tiddlywinks.

Half-heartedly she pushed the chair against the coatroom door and climbed up. All she could see through the low transom was a wriggling bundle of assorted clothing.

"That's Amy with the green sweater."

No response.

"Then that's Agatha under the plaid coat now."

There was more quivering in the bundle—as if a dozen cats were hiding in a sack.

"Mabel's under that black cape or whatever it is."

Still no response.

Luvvy was disgusted with the game. She never should have let them entice her into it. She should have written a letter home. She waited hesitantly for a few silent moments.

She quietly stepped down from the chair and tip-toed away. If they enjoyed being locked up in a closet, let them stay there for a good long time. Let them sweat and suffocate in the coatroom until they figured out what had happened.

She left the playroom and went outside. She took deep breaths of the fresh fall air.

Hetty was still sitting on the tree bench with the portfolio on her knees, so there was no use in trying to chat with her. Betsey and her book had disappeared.

Luvvy had a new idea of how to pass time quickly. She could begin writing the story she had been think-ing about. She went upstairs to her empty classroom

and got a tablet and pencil from her desk. She would do her writing on the bench in the corner of the porch so the girls wouldn't be able to see her when they came from the playroom. Let them look for *her* now.

She began her story. "Oliver Ambruster was the present master of the old Claiborne plantation. His face was dark, stern and harsh. He had jet black eye-brows under a lock of raven black hair. He glowered at his beautiful wife, Camilla." Luvvy glowered a little herself. Was he too much like Rochester in *Jane Eyre?*

She had already thought out most of the plot. It was to be a tragedy. Oliver was jealous of his wife because she came from an aristocratic southern family and he had been a poor boy. Even the plantation on which they lived belonged to Camilla's family. For spite, Oliver was going to give their two children away to his cruel sister.

Mama had read a book in which that happened, and that was why she was in sympathy with the suf-fragettes who were trying to get the vote for women. But Papa was against them. "Next thing the women will be wearing pants and taking men's jobs," he had said. "But not in my factory—not by a damn sight." Of course Papa hadn't read the book, and he never, never would have given his children away anyhow.

To return to the star-crossed Ambrusters. Crazed by grief, Camilla pulled her father's Civil War sword from its scabbard and stabbed Oliver to death.

Luvvy raised her eyes to the highest porch on the adjoining wing of the convent. She could almost see crazed Camilla standing there with a bloody sword in her hand. Her eyes were wild and her velvet gown disheveled. (Was that pronounced dis-heveled or di-sheveled?) With an agonizing cry, Camilla leaped over the railing and plummeted to the walkway below —narrowly missing Sister Veronica who was coming from the nuns' garden to take her turn at the front door.

"The Vengeance of the Sword" would be a good name for the story when it was finished. She would copy it neatly in ink and send it to the *Ladies' Home Journal*. She was too old now to be writing for the children's page of the *Baltimore Sunday Sun*.

Four o'clock chimes floated over the convent gar-den. They sounded melancholy and regretful. "Ding, dong, ding, dong, too late, too late. Ding, dong, ding, dong, don't wait, don't wait."

Maybe Papa had some punctures along the way to delay them. It always took so long for him to mend a tire by the roadside. Raising the wheel with the jack, finding the puncture, and mending it with one of the patches he carried in a tin box under the front seat was a lengthy operation. One time when they had driven to Baltimore, there had been eleven punctures, and they had turned homeward even though the "clustered spires" of Baltimore had been visible in the distance. But Papa surely wouldn't turn back if he were so close to Frederick.

While she sat staring into space, Betsey and Mary Leary came out of the dormitory door.

"We're going down to the library room to get some books to read," said Betsey. "I finished mine. Don't you want to come too?"

She might as well. She really knew that there hadn't been any punctures. They weren't coming this Sunday, and it would be a whole week until another Sunday. She might as well get a book to read. It would be more interesting than her own story, because she wouldn't know what was coming next.

The library was a handsome room with glossy floors and dark wood paneling. There were marble statues on pedestals, potted palms, and rows of glass-doored bookcases. It was the kind of a room in which Camilla Ambruster would stab her husband.

Luvvy feasted her eyes on the books. It was such a difficult decision to make. Encyclopedias and biographies of saints. Muhlbach's volumes of historical fiction looked inviting. She was trying to decide between *Empress Josephine* and *Marie Antoinette and Her Son* when she felt a hand on her shoulder. She looked up to see Sister Mary Clare smiling at her.

"Here's a story you will love," said Sister. "It is more appropriate than those."

She put a book in Luvvy's hand. The title written in gilt letters within a garland of gilded lilies was *Agnes of the Lilies*.

"You will find that little Agnes has all the virtues that girls your age would do well to imitate," said Sister.

Luvvy had a foreboding that Agnes wasn't going to be half as interesting as the Empress Josephine or Marie Antoinette. But she wanted to please her teacher.

"Thank you, Sister," she said. "I'll read some of it tonight because I won't have anything else to do." She was certain that none of the girls would want to play with her for awhile. And she was sure that she didn't want to play with them. Hide-and-seek in a closet. Ugh!

She read the book until the supper bell rang. Her suspicion was well-founded. It was a dull, preachy book.

When the bell rang she fell into line with the other girls.

"What happened to you?" asked Eunice, glowering as darkly as Oliver Ambruster. "We waited a donkey's age in that coatroom."

The line began to move into the refectory so Luvvy didn't have to make any explanation. But once they were seated at the table, Agatha giggled and said, "You sure played a good joke on us, Luvvy."

Amy looked at her reproachfully. "It was a very unkind joke. It was downright uncharitable. I wouldn't do such a thing to my friends, would you?" She appealed to Mabel.

"I think it was a mean trick," agreed Mabel. "We shouldn't even talk to her."

"Oh, fudge!" exclaimed Agatha. "It was funny— with nobody wanting to look out the door first for fear it was a trick so Luvvy could catch her."

From then on only Agatha would admit that Luvvy was at the table. It was humiliating to Luvvy to have poor, homely Agatha championing her. She looked at the empty space across. If only Mary Letitia would get here. Then she would have a real friend. They would have so much in common—horses and fields and country life. She ate her biscuit and thinly sliced ham silently, ignoring Agatha's attempts to include her in the conversation. At least the food was good.

It took three days to write "The Vengeance of the Sword" and four to read *Agnes of the Lilies*. Ordinarily Luvvy was a fast reader, but Agnes was such a dull, disappointing heroine.

She was a saintly child being raised by the nuns in the convent because she was an orphan. Agatha Mulcahy was in the same situation, but she wasn't goody-goody like the book's heroine. Agnes never did anything wrong. When she could have been playing with other children, she went to the chapel to pray. It took her two whole chapters to die, and she kept begging to be buried with the nuns in their little cemetery with lilies blooming on her grave.

Luvvy doggedly followed Agnes all the way to the graveside because Sister Mary Clare had once said that not finishing a book one had begun showed weak character.

"How did you like the book I gave you?" asked Sister Mary Clare after class one day. "Wasn't it inspiring?"

"It was all right," answered Luvvy without enthusiasm.

"Don't you think little Agnes was a saint?"

"Uh-huh! I mean yes, Sister. But she didn't seem real. I guess it's because I've never known any saints." Luvvy really thought that Agnes was an insufferable prig.

That afternoon Luvvy got pen and ink to copy her own story of "The Vengeance of the Sword" neatly for the *Ladies' Home Journal*. She reread the scribbled pages critically. Oliver Ambruster was as evil as little Agnes had been good. She really had never known anyone so wicked. And she had never known any woman capable of stabbing her husband to death. Mama had been so grief-stricken after Maudie's death that she had taken to her bed and almost become an invalid, but she hadn't jumped off the upstairs porch.

Was anybody in her story real? Luvvy decided not.

She slowly tore the pages into scraps, then threw them into a trash basket.

Later when Betsey asked, "Was that book about Agnes and the lilies any good?" Luvvy hotly declared, "I hate little Agnes. She wasn't true at all. Even Amy Ackroyd isn't that good. And I hate the Ambrusters too."

"Who are the Ambrusters?" asked Betsey. "I don't know any Ambrusters."

"Neither do I," admitted Luvvy. "They're just some silly characters in a story I wrote, but I've thrown it away."

6.

Mary Letitia

It was a Sunday to remember for weeks after.

"They're here! They're here!" cried Betsey, racing across the grass in defiance of the rules. Thus must someone have alerted Barbara Fritchie on that long-remembered September day.

Luvvy was giddy with surprise and happiness. Betsey's excitement could only mean that the family had come at last. She followed Betsey to the parlor. Sister Veronica did not reprimand them for their unladylike haste. She knew the reason for it since she had just opened the outside parlor door to the Savage family from Weverton.

Luvvy was nearly hysterical as she rushed from

Mama to Papa to Regina to little Marylou for a hug and kiss.

Hetty was already there, sitting sedately on one of the stiff chairs. Such a lively family made the parlor look almost habitable. Most of the time the mohair-covered sofa and the geometrically spaced chairs were empty, with a smell of furniture polish and piety pervading the atmosphere. Even the inevitable potted palm usually looked artificial.

Now there was life and chatter. Already Papa was profaning the air with a big brown cigar. Since he was twenty years older than Mama, his hair was beginning to gray and he spent less time at his factory in Hagerstown. "If I can't make a living for my family after ten o'clock, I sure as blazes can't before then."

"And I suppose you want to be a nun now," he teased Luvvy.

Luvvy thought to herself, No, I want to go home. But everybody was so gay and happy that she didn't think this the time to mention it.

"How do you like boarding-school life?" Mama asked her. She was a short, plump woman, with blue-black hair parted in the middle and twinkling dimples.

"She's doing well in her studies, Mama Della," Hetty answered for her, "and all the nuns like her."

The nuns, not the girls.

"The nuns are real nice," said Luvvy. "I made a

hundred on my last English test, and Sister Mary Clare gave me a holy card."

Curly-headed Marylou, sitting shyly beside Mama with her thumb in her mouth, said, "I want a holy card."

She was a pretty little child with blue eyes and lips that usually looked puckered for a kiss.

"I'll get you one," offered Regina. "I do want to go inside and see some of my old friends. Do you want to come with me, any of you?"

Regina had graduated only that June, so she still had strong ties with some of the girls. Luvvy thought that she looked more beautiful than ever with her silky hair and "Grecian nose," as everyone in the family described it.

"I've been seeing your old friends for the past weeks," said Betsey, "so I'm staying here."

"I'll go with you," offered Hetty.

Luvvy suspected that Hetty really wanted to get Regina alone to ask about Alec.

Those in the parlor talked about what was going on at home.

Valley's colt, Sassy, had been sold to the Stone-brakers.

Old Mr. Johnson, the Civil War veteran, had died, and people from miles around had come to the funeral.

The German butcher in Knoxville had put up a sign in his shop saying, "No War Talk In Here."

Everyone was happy that President Wilson was going to marry Mrs. Galt. The poor man had been so lonely since his first wife's death. And it was fitting for a man his age to marry a widow.

Just as Luvvy had gained enough courage to ask if she could go home with them, there was a rustle and movement behind the grating that separated the clois-tered part of the parlor from that of visitors. Since the Visitandines were cloistered, they always remained behind the grating.

Mother Mary Austin had come to greet the family. She reached fingers through the grating to clasp those of each of the visitors in turn, then drew up a chair.

"We are so pleased to have Luvena with us this year," said Mother. "I have fine reports about her work and deportment." She pushed back a side of her veil and smiled at Luvvy. "Perhaps she will see fit to join us one day since Regina didn't."

Luvvy was as frightened as if she were about to be kidnapped. She moved closer to Mama.

"I don't think I want to be a nun, Reverend Mother," she said. "I—I wouldn't want to cut my hair off."

That brought a polite laugh from Mother Mary Austin.

Fearing she might have offended her, Luvvy added, "But I like being a pupil here."

Now she had committed herself. She couldn't go home yet.

When Hetty returned with Regina, Mother Mary Austin squeezed fingers again and assured them that they were always remembered in the nuns' prayers. Then she slipped away like a shadow.

Papa took his big gold watch with the stag engraved on the case from his pocket. He said it was time to leave because fresh gravel had been put on some of the roads, which heightened the danger of punctures.

Luvvy hugged and kissed them in turn, blinking back the tears. If only she could go back with them, she wouldn't care if they had as many punctures as on that Baltimore trip.

It seemed so lonely with them gone. She had never even felt that lonely when she was waiting for them to come and they didn't.

As she disconsolately wandered out on the porch again, she saw a group of her classmates excitedly pointing to the sky. She looked up to see a man dangling from a parachute high above.

Luvvy raced down the steps and joined the girls.

"You missed it," cried Agatha. "He jumped out of a balloon, but it's gone now."

"He must belong to the Fall Fair," said Mabel. "I wish we could go to it."

It looked as if man and parachute were directly above them.

"Oh, I wish he'd land on the ground here," cried Luvvy. "Wouldn't that be thrilling?"

"The nuns wouldn't allow it," said Mabel. "They don't let any man in here but the workmen—and the relatives during Commencement Week."

"But they couldn't stop him," Luvvy pointed out. She squeezed her hands together. "Let's pray that he does land here."

Amy disapproved. "It wouldn't be right to pray for such a thing," she said. "It might even be a venial sin."

But Luvvy was sure that Amy wanted it to happen too.

They watched the slow descent hopefully. But as it lowered, the parachute seemed to be drifting away. It floated farther and farther from the convent until it was no bigger than a gnat, and disappeared beyond the bakehouse.

The girls were full of gloom, but Luvvy had an encouraging idea.

"I'm going to write a love story about a man coming down with a parachute and landing in some beautiful girl's garden," she announced. "I know about parachutes now that I've seen one."

The girls went to the nearest porch stairs and sat down. Luvvy stayed with them for lack of anything better to do. She buried her chin in her hands and began thinking about what would happen when the strange man landed in the beautiful girl's garden.

"Look who's coming!" cried Mabel suddenly.

It was Sister Mary Cecilia leading a strange girl by the hand. She was a chubby girl with long taffy-colored hair held back from her forehead by a wide green ribbon that matched her green suit.

"Mary Letitia Moore!" cried Mabel. "I bet it's Mary Letitia."

A flutter of excitement went through the group. With Luvvy it was like a charge of electricity. Mary Letitia was here at last. She was glad that she hadn't gone home. Boarding school life would become as enjoyable as she had assured Mother Mary Austin it already was.

The pair came slowly toward the girls on the steps. They jumped up. Luvvy had a sudden stroke of shyness. But she smiled broadly at the new girl.

It all seemed so unreal that Mary Letitia's introduction to the girls was like some play Luvvy was seeing over again.

Sister Mary Cecilia: Girls, I want you to meet little Mary Letitia Moore. It is unfortunate that she has arrived late, but I know you will make her feel at home. Mary Letitia, this is Amy Ackroyd and Agatha Mulcahy. And here are Luvena Savage and Mabel Courtney—some of our nicest girls.

Mary Letitia: It's so nice to meet you all. I know I'll

be very happy here. That's what Mama and
Papa said.

Sister Mary Cecilia: I must go back to the parlor to
assure Mary Letitia's parents that their daughter
is now in good hands. Amy, will you be responsible for Mary Letitia?

Mary Letitia: Thank you, Sister. That's very thoughtful of you.

Amy (with angelic smile): I'll take good care of her,
Sister. Mary Letitia, shall we take a little walk
around the grounds so we can get better acquainted? You'll excuse us for a few minutes,
won't you, girls?

Mary Letitia: I enjoyed meeting you. I'll see you all
soon again.

Luvvy was bitterly disappointed. Why hadn't Sister chosen her to look after Mary Letitia? She was
disappointed in the new girl too. She sounded like a
talking doll.

But that's the way I talked when I first came, she
remembered with surprise. She's shy and doesn't really
know what to say. But she won't be like that when
she knows me better and we talk about horses.

"Why don't we go to the bread box and get something to eat?" suggested Agatha.

The bread box was the open window of the refectory where one of the domestic nuns in white veil

handed out slices of buttered bread in the afternoon.

Since they were sprinkled with sugar this time, Luvvy asked for two pieces. The sugar lifted mere bread into the cake class. She should have told Mama about it. She was sure that Marylou would love such a treat.

As she munched the bread, she could see Amy and Mary Letitia slowly walking along the path. The play she had imagined continued, but she had to make up the dialogue herself now.

Mary Letitia: All the girls seem nice.

Amy: They really are. Agatha Mulcahy is particularly nice but she's very poor. She's a charity student and that's my old dress she's wearing. I like to help the poor, don't you?

Mary Letitia: I don't know. I've never known any poor people.

Amy: Naturally you wouldn't, but now you know Agatha. Shall we sit down on this bench.

(*They sit.*)

Mary Letitia: And what about Luvena Savage? I liked her especially.

Amy: We don't know her very well because she stays with her sisters most of the time. I wouldn't hang around my older sisters all the time, would you?

Mary Letitia: I don't know. I don't have any sisters,

only a little brother. But perhaps Luvena doesn't share the same interests as you all. Now I love horses, do you?

Amy: Horses? Goodness, no. I wouldn't know a horse's tail from its mane. I love butterflies. I made a collection of them on our plantation this summer—we own a plantation on the eastern shore, you know. But my kitten ruined them.

Agatha pulled down the curtain on Luvvy's imagined play.

"What are you grinning about?" she asked. "What's so funny?"

Luvvy was flustered. "Oh, I was just thinking about a joke I read one time."

"That's an idea," said Agatha. "Eunice has a new book of jokes and riddles. Want to get it, Eunice?"

Jokes and riddles! "What's black and white and red all over?" "Why did the hen cross the road?" How long would it be until she would have a chance to talk to Mary Letitia? It looked as if she and Amy were permanently glued to that bench.

"Some other time, Agatha," said Luvvy. "Betsey said she'd help me with some arithmetic problems, and I think I see her up on the porch now."

It wasn't until supper that Luvvy was with Mary Letitia again. The empty place at the table was filled at last.

The girls were still giggling and laughing about the riddle book.

"Some of you weren't with us," said Mabel. "Let's ask them some of the riddles and see if they know the answers. Why do little pigs eat so much?"

"Because they have bad manners?" asked Amy.

"No."

"I don't know," said Luvvy. Silly riddle. She didn't even care what the answer was. She wished she could work horses into the conversation instead of pigs.

Since Mary Letitia had nothing to offer, Eunice said, "They all want to make hogs of themselves."

The girls laughed uproariously.

"Here's another," said Eunice. "When you go to bed what's the last thing you take off?"

"Your hair ribbon?" asked Mary Letitia.

"No."

"Your bloomers," said Luvvy.

Amy was shocked. "That's not decent," she reproved.

"I don't think it's decent to sleep in your bloomers," said Luvvy.

Eunice quickly explained, "The last thing you take off is your feet off the floor."

More laughter.

Mabel had another one. "What is taller sitting down than standing up."

"Sister Margaret Mary," said Luvvy. She was the

nun who sat on a high platform in the study room.

"No, it's a dog. And here's a good one. Thirty white horses on a red hill, now they stamp, now they champ, now they stand still. What are they?"

Luvvy dropped her fork on her plate. Here was her opening at last. She leaned toward Mary Letitia.

"I love horses," she declared, although she still had some food in her mouth.

"Papa does too," said Mary Letitia. "He has some race horses. Two of them are in the races at the Fair."

"But you haven't tried to answer the riddle yet," protested Mabel. "What are the white horses?"

"Teeth," answered Luvvy impatiently. "I've heard that one a dozen times. Do you ever ride the race horses, Mary Letitia?"

"Oh, no. Only the trainer and the jockeys ride them."

"I guess you have your own riding horse," suggested Luvvy. "Maybe a Kentucky Thoroughbred. Ours are only carriage horses, but they're used to the saddle too."

Mary Letitia shook her head. "No."

"Then you must have a pony," persisted Luvvy. "Hetty and Betsey had a pony years ago. They even brought him into the house sometimes."

"Roger—he's my brother—he has a pony, but I won't go near Dandy. He bites and kicks sometimes. And I'm even more afraid of horses. I would

70

never be brave enough to get up on one."

"What *do* you like to do for fun?" asked Luvvy desperately. "Write stories or poetry?"

"Not unless I have to for my governess," said Mary Letitia. "I like to paint on china. I'm finishing a tea set for Mama for a Christmas present."

Amy seized the conversation which Luvvy immediately dropped. "How artistic! I've always wanted to learn how. I'll ask my mother if I can take lessons next summer."

"I'd be happy to teach you if you want to visit me," offered Mary Letitia.

Luvvy couldn't remember that Amy had ever mentioned any interest in painting china. But she felt no envy at her invitation to visit the other girl. Luvvy had lost all interest in Mary Letitia as a best friend. You never could depend on girls outside your own family. They always turned out to be a disappointment. She wished she had gone home in the Machine.

7.

Weeds in the Garden

It was Amy's idea.

"Wasn't that an inspiring sermon we had in chapel this morning?" she asked the other girls. "That our vices are like weeds in the beautiful garden of our virtues, and that we should try to uproot them."

"How can we have any vices when the nuns are always watching us?" asked Mabel.

Amy looked at her reprovingly. "You didn't really get his message then," she said. "Father meant that we all have little imperfections in our characters, and that we should try to overcome them."

There was no comment so Amy continued, "I've thought of something that might help us. Why don't we each tell the other her worst fault? It would really be the kind thing to do."

"Somebody might get mad," said Agatha. "I might."

"Now, Agatha, how could you be angry with someone who is trying to help you? That would be ungrateful."

"I know what," said Mabel. "Let's each hold up her hand and make a vow not to get mad."

One by one, they held up a hand and solemnly swore, "I vow I will not be offended by having my faults brought to light."

This was going to be worse than hide-and-seek in the coatroom, thought Luvvy. But she was curious to learn what they found wrong with her. Probably that she acted too old for her age. She didn't think that a vice, but they were so childish they probably would.

"We'll begin with Agatha," said Amy. "Agatha, you giggle too much. It's very irritating."

The others agreed.

"I don't think that's a vice," objected Agatha.

"I think Agatha giggles because she has a sense of humor and the rest of you don't," said Luvvy.

They scowled at her.

"What's wrong with me?" asked Mabel.

"You're frivolous," accused Eunice.

"What do you mean 'frivolous?' "

"You don't give enough attention to serious

things," put in Amy. "You fritter your time when you should be studying."

"That's why you get such poor marks," added Eunice.

"If I want to fritter, that's my own business," snapped Mabel. "And I think you're all frittery."

Luvvy thought this exchange most frittering.

Amy accused, "Eunice is vain."

"Why do you say that?" asked Eunice in an injured voice.

"Every time you pass a mirror you look into it," explained Amy. "You're always looking at your reflection in the store windows when we go downtown Saturdays."

The others nodded.

"I do not," said Eunice hotly. Her eyes stared even more.

"What's my fault?" Mary Letitia asked. "I really know because Mama is always telling me."

"We won't say anything about you," said Amy graciously, "because we don't know you well enough yet."

"Then I'll tell you what it is," confided Mary Letitia. "I'm a slowpoke. That's what Mama says. And it's so hard here to get dressed in fifteen minutes. I'm always late getting into line."

"Perhaps it's because you're so thorough," Amy excused her.

Luvvy thought Mary Letitia's worst fault was that she was such a scaredy-cat she was even afraid of ponies.

Amy turned to her. "And I hate to say this, Luvvy, but you're stuck-up."

"I am not," declared Luvvy. "I never was stuck-up."

Eunice tried to explain. "It isn't that you're exactly stuck-up. It's just that you seem to feel superior to us."

"As if you think we aren't good enough for you," added Mabel.

"I don't think Luvvy's stuck-up and superior," said Agatha. "She's just hard to know."

Luvvy was indignant. "You think you're so perfect, Amy Ackroyd," she exploded. "I'll tell you what's wrong with you. You're a goody-goody. You're like little Agnes in a boring book I read."

Amy looked wounded. "Doesn't everyone try to be good?"

"You try too hard," declared Luvvy. "You're a hypocrite."

To her astonishment, Amy burst into tears. Mary Letitia put her arm around her.

"Don't cry, Amy," she tried to console her. "I think you're the sweetest girl I've ever met."

But the other girls looked at Luvvy approvingly.

"Remember we vowed we wouldn't be offended

75

by any criticism," Agatha reminded them.

When they sat down to supper that evening, it was apparent that more than one had been offended. Mabel was unusually quiet, and Eunice looked down-right sullen. Amy had the expression of a martyred saint on her face. Luvvy had already decided not to speak to any of them ever again. She wouldn't return to the convent after Christmas vacation.

There was a stir among the tables as Sister Marie Jeanne d'Arc entered the refectory. Something important must have brought her there. Had somebody been skipping French class?

She folded her arms in her wide sleeves and waited for silence.

"I have come to inform you of a new rule for the refectory, girls," she announced. "From now on only French will be spoken at meals. Reverend Mother thinks that will improve your conversational French."

Eunice's silence spread over the whole room. There was only the twitter of some Big Girls at a nearby table who had already had years of French. Sister Marie Jeanne d'Arc walked between the tables to see that the rule was obeyed.

Amy broke the silence at their table by requesting Agatha, "*Passez le pain, s'il vous plaît.*"

Agatha stared at her blankly.

Mabel nudged her. "*Le* bread, Agatha. *Et s'il vous plâit, passez le beurre—le* butter."

Agatha giggled. *"Bon jour, pain,"* she said as she picked up the bread dish. *"Au revoir, beurre"* as she passed the butter.

Luvvy said nothing. She hadn't had enough French lessons to ask for anything. And she didn't want anything more. Acting superior indeed! Amy was the one who was always acting superior. But they had all agreed with Amy—all but Agatha. That showed how childish they were.

That night Luvvy tiptoed into Betsey's curtain to tell her troubles and win sympathy.

"I'm certainly glad to have you and Hetty here," she said, "or I wouldn't stay in this place another day."

"What's wrong now?" asked Betsey.

"Those silly little girls. Today that goody Amy suggested we should tell each other our faults. But it was Amy who did most of the telling."

Betsey laughed. "We did that one time but it ended up with everybody mad. Mary Leary and I wouldn't speak to each other for a whole day."

Luvvy couldn't imagine Betsey and Mary having a spat. Her curiosity made her momentarily forget her own indignation.

"What did you tell each other?" she asked.

"I told Mary that she was gawky—always bumping into things and falling down stairs, and she said I had a temper."

"But you do," said Luvvy. "Remember that time Regina and Hetty locked you out of the bedroom and you kicked the door so hard you broke the lock?"

Betsey laughed again. "I guess we can't see our own faults," she admitted.

"But do you know what they said about *me*?" Luvvy asked. "That I'm stuck-up. That's not true."

"You're not stuck-up," agreed Betsey.

"But that's not all. They said I feel superior to them."

"Don't you? You just called them silly."

"They are. They're always thinking of silly things to do. No wonder I'd rather be with you and Hetty."

"Then you really do feel superior to them, don't you?"

"Oh, I guess so," Luvvy grudgingly admitted.

"You'll never make friends that way. You've really been very unfriendly, Luvvy. I've noticed it all along. You won't always be with your family. What will you do alone without friends?"

Tears came to Luvvy's eyes. Even Betsey was against her. Everybody here at the convent was against her. She angrily yanked the curtain open and left.

She jumped into bed and pulled the covers over her head. She tried to fall asleep as fast as she could, but her confused thoughts kept her awake.

Wasn't what Betsey said true? The Little Girls

did try to include her in their games, but she often rebuffed their friendly advances. And what would happen when Betsey and Hetty grew up and left home as Regina was planning to do?

She went back to Betsey's curtain and poked her head through.

"Goodnight, Betsey," she whispered. "I'll think about what you said."

The French meals went on for a few more days. There was little conversation at the tables. Sister Marie Jeanne d'Arc no longer appeared in the refectory since everything seemed to be going smoothly.

One evening, Agatha grinned mischievously and suggested, "Ets-lay alk-tay ig-pay atin-lay."

Let's talk pig latin! You took the consonant or consonant blend beginning a word, moved it to the end and added "ay." Luvvy had tried to teach it to Maudie one time without success.

She was eager to be more friendly with the girls.

"Es-yay, es-yay," she agreed. "I-ay ike-lay ig-pay atin-lay."

Amy admonished, "O-nay, o-nay. I mean—" She clapped her hands over her mouth. "*C'est defendu.*"

The others paid no attention to her warning that it was forbidden. Agatha and Eunice were able to talk pig latin so fast that it did sound like a foreign language. Almost like French, with all the "ay" sounds.

"I-ay ate-hay ench-Fray."

"And-ay I-ay ate-hay is-thay ew-stay."

"Ease-play ass-pay e-thay alt-say and-ay epper-pay."

Luvvy was no longer angry with them for trying to uproot her weed of vice. Even Betsey had agreed with them. She would be friendly and try to mend her ways. They had already forgiven each other.

"O-day ou-yay ink-thay igs-pay alk-tay eir-they atin-lay?" she asked Agatha.

Agatha didn't answer. The frozen look on her face was a warning. The whole table had suddenly fallen silent. Luvvy sensed Sister Marie Jeanne d'Arc's presence before she heard her stern voice.

"And just what foreign language are you girls speaking?" she asked, moving to Luvvy's table. "It's not French. It's not Spanish. I doubt that it is even Chinese."

Luvvy gulped. "It's pig latin, Sister," she confessed.

Agatha remembered the rule. "C'est le latin des porcs, ma soeur."

Sister Marie Jeanne d'Arc's glance sliced across the table. "And how many of you have been using this vulgar gibberish instead of the beautiful French language?"

Everyone raised a hand.

"You will each sit on the penance bench for half an hour after this meal," Sister sentenced them.

The meal was finished in gloomy silence.

Dutifully they filed out into the yard and arranged themselves on a long hard bench, making an unbroken row of black aprons. They sat staring across the hedge, watching the nuns walking back and forth in their garden as they read their evening prayers.

Luvvy soon felt restless so she began composing a jingle in her head.

> *The girl sat on the penance bench*
> *Whence all but she had been excused.*
> *She sat there hour after hour*
> *Unrepentant and bemused.*

She would tell it to the girls when their penance was over.

Two Big Girls sauntered past arm in arm. They smirked at the penitents.

"Look at the little flock of blackbirds perched on the bench," said one with a snicker. "*Les petits oiseaux noirs.*"

"No, they're Latin piglets," said the other. "Oink-ay, oink-ay, oink-ay."

But Luvvy didn't mind their teasing. She really had come to feel like one of the Little Girls now, and it was a warm pleasant feeling.

The very next morning Sister Marie Jeanne d'Arc appeared in the refectory again. Who had broken the rule now?

"Girls," she said, "Reverend Mother has withdrawn the rule for speaking only French at meals. Upon further consideration, she fears that it may interfere with your conversational graces." She fixed her glance upon Luvvy's table. "But for obvious reasons, no porcine Latin will be permitted."

This ended the fun of pig latin, especially since everyone at Luvvy's table had become so fluent with it. The refectory became filled with the buzz of conversational graces.

Thanksgiving came, with its boxes from home filled with cakes, cookies, and candies.

Everyone was mostly thankful that Christmas vacation would be next. All the girls were talking about it except Agatha. She quietly listened to the others.

"We'll go to the plantation and have a real old-fashioned Christmas," Amy informed them.

"I do hope I'll get a fur muff and tippet this year," said Eunice.

"I finished the tea set for Mama," announced Mary Letitia. "I know she'll be pleased." Lucky Mary Letitia sometimes went home over the weekend because her estate was so close to Frederick.

A month, just three weeks, only two weeks—then *one* week until vacation. Luvvy could almost believe in Santa Claus.

8.
Clay, Junior

Christmas vacation went by so fast that it seemed to Luvvy like a beautiful dream. She was now awake and back in school.

Sister Mary Clare said, "Girls, now that vacation is over, I want each of you to write a composition entitled 'My Christmas Vacation.' Then you will read them aloud in class. In that way, you will share your happy experiences with each other."

Although Luvvy didn't usually like assigned topics, this one pleased her. It would give her the chance to relive the precious holidays. As she raced her pencil over the page, she was back in Shady Grove. She hadn't remained there, as she had often planned, and she would tell why in the composition.

My Christmas Vacation

Although I've lived a long time, each Christmas seems like the first one in the world to me. We always go into the mountains and chop down a pretty pine tree. We have to be careful when we light the candles on it so they won't cause a fire. Mama keeps a bucket of water near the tree when it is lighted.

Santa Claus comes to our house on Christmas Eve. We wait for him after supper. Marylou keeps asking, "When is he coming? Why isn't he here yet?" He couldn't come until after dark because he had to feed the horses and milk the cows first. Our new farm-hand, Charlie Stevens, was Santa Claus. Mama had to stuff him with a lot of pillows because he is so skinny.

I received a silver comb and brush set, a Parcheesi game, a book called "Pilgrim's Progress" which is very boring, a stocking cap, two boxes of stationery, some lily-of-the-valley perfume, an embroidered pillow top, a pencil box, and six handkerchiefs. I already have thirty-nine.

We all stayed up for Midnight Mass—all but Mary-lou. She was happy to go to bed with her new teddy bear. We drove to Brunswick for Midnight Mass.

Our church was full of candlelight and organ music and sleepy people. I think I was the sleepiest because I fell asleep twice. The last hymn makes everybody wide

85

awake because it is so fast and loud and everybody sings it. Father O'Connell made up the words himself. It goes like this:

> And it tells a wondrous story of a Child, of a
> Child
> Meek and mild, meek and mild, undefiled, un-
> defiled.
> And it tells a wondrous story as we go, as we go,
> To and fro, to and fro, meek and mo, meek and
> mo.

Mama thinks that Father O'Connell should have been a poet, but Papa says he makes a better priest.

Christmas Day I played Parcheesi and went horseback riding. Other than that, there was nothing to do but eat a big dinner.

The rest of the week, I rode horseback on Valley most of the time. Parcheesi gets boring, too.

Right after Christmas, the young people in Sandy Hook, the village near Harpers Ferry, dress up in funny costumes and masks and visit the farmhouses around. Papa calls them mummers.

First we heard an awful noise in the yard. They were screeching and banging on tin pans. Mama went to the door and invited them in. The mummers are the most fun of all, although Marylou was more scared of them than Santa Claus.

Most of the men dress in women's clothes, and some of the women wear trousers. Their faces are blackened or covered with masks, and we have to try to guess who they are. You ask them questions, and they answer in high, squeaky voices so you won't know them. I recognized Pansy, Marylou's nurse, right away because she was wearing my old sunbonnet. After we had guessed some of them, Mama served them eggnog and cake.

It started snowing one day. Mama had Charlie hitch Dolly to the sleigh and she took us for a ride to Weverton. The sleigh bells sounded so jolly. Before we got back, the sun came out and the snow turned to mud. We all had to get out and push the sleigh to help Dolly pull it home. The sleigh bells didn't sound jolly anymore.

It was New Year's Eve too soon, because that meant we would soon be going back to school. I always want to see the New Year in with the others but, as usual, I fell asleep before midnight.

When I first went home, I was so happy to be with my family and the horses that I thought I would stay and not come back here. Then Hetty and Betsey kept talking about the fun we had at the convent. Betsey made everything that had happened to us seem funny or exciting. She even laughed about the Saturday she had to sit on the penance bench for eating a pickle on the street. She didn't think it was funny then.

I really began to miss school the way I missed home for so long. When I told Mama about all the things we Little Girls had done together, they really did sound funny or exciting. I wonder why things seem different when they're over.

Happy Christmas to all, and to all a good morning.

After class, Agatha sought her out. "You always

have such a good time at home," she said, "but I'm glad you did come back."

"But you had a good time here at the convent," said Luvvy. "You told in your composition how the nuns made a special Christmas tree for you. And that Sister Veronica even took you over to the Monastery once."

"It isn't like being with your own family in a real home," said Agatha.

Luvvy began to wonder about something.

"I thought maybe Amy would take you home with her for the holidays since you're such good friends. Her Christmas on their plantation sounded so nice and old-fashioned with the roast goose and plum pudding."

"Oh, I couldn't expect that. Holidays are a family time."

That was true. At Christmas you wanted to be with your own family without outsiders.

Nearly a month afterward, Luvvy had reason to regret that she hadn't stayed home after Christmas vacation.

The great event that she had been expecting for so long suddenly happened. Like all things one has been awaiting so long, it seemed as if it never would happen. And it was the kind of thing one didn't talk about outside one's family. It would have shocked Amy if Luvvy had talked to the Little Girls about it.

The eighth grade was studying Maryland in geography class.

Amy recited in one long breath that ran out at the end, "Maryland is bounded on the north by Pennsylvania, on the east by Delaware, the Atlantic and a small part of Virginia, south and west by the District of Columbia and the Potomac, and on the extreme west by West Virginia."

Luvvy hoped Sister would ask her to name the counties. Many of them had such beautiful names that rolled off the tongue like those in a ballad. Queen Anne. Prince George. Caroline. Anne Arundel. If she ever had a daughter, she would name her Anne Arundel after the wife of the second Lord Baltimore.

She heard the girls in back rising from their desks so she looked around to see who was entering the classroom. She half expected to see Anne Arundel herself in satins and laces.

It was only Sister Veronica. She was apologetic and motioned the girls to take their seats again.

"May I speak to Luvena in private?" she asked Sister Mary Clare. "It is very important."

Luvvy followed her into the hall with misgivings. What was wrong now? She hadn't eaten her cone last Saturday, and she certainly hadn't eaten anything on the street.

"Luvena, you have a brother," announced Sister Veronica.

For a second, Luvvy thought Sister must have her mixed up with Mary Letitia. She didn't have a brother.

"The telegram just came," continued Sister Veronica. "A dear little brother was born to your dear mother last night."

Luvvy gave a squeal of joy. Of course that's what it was. Hadn't she been waiting endless months for this news? And it had come finding her completely unprepared.

"Congratulations!" said Sister Veronica. "God has sent you a dear little brother to take the place of the sister He took from you. You may go into the chapel to say a prayer of thanksgiving. I will explain your absence to Sister Mary Clare."

"Is Mama all right?" asked Luvvy. "Do Hetty and Betsey know?"

"Your dear mother is in fine health and so is your father. Your sisters are already praying in the chapel."

Luvvy hurried to join them.

"Do you think they'll bring him to see us next Sunday?" she whispered to Betsey. "Who do you think he looks like?"

"Sh-h-h!" warned Betsey. "We're supposed to pray now."

Luvvy found that hard to do. Oh, how she wished

she had stayed home after Christmas. She remembered how much larger Mama had grown and how slowly she had moved around.

"Do you think they'll let us go home to see him?" Luvvy whispered to Hetty.

"Sh-h-h!" whispered Hetty. "Pray."

Luvvy prayed that they could go home, or that Papa and Mama would bring the new baby to the convent next Sunday.

The Little Girls were almost as excited as Luvvy.

"Aren't you lucky!" exclaimed Agatha. "I'd be satisfied to have a baby sister, since I'm the only one left in my family."

"How much does he weigh?" asked Eunice.

"Seven pounds and five ounces," replied Luvvy. "That's what the telegram said."

"My brother weighed almost nine pounds when he was born," boasted Mary Letitia.

"Has he been baptized yet?" asked Amy.

"I don't think so," replied Luvvy. "They'll prob-ably wait until we get home."

"But that won't be until Easter vacation. It's important to have a baby baptized as soon as possible."

Just when Luvvy was beginning to feel like one of the Little Girls, she found that now she had less time for them. She wanted to be with her sisters to talk about their new brother. Only those in her family could understand how wonderful it was to have a boy, after six girls.

"What do you think they'll name him?" she asked her sisters. "Oh, I wish it would be something like Howard or Frederick." She was still thinking about the lovely names of the counties of Maryland.

"Probably Clay Junior," said Hetty.

One thing was certain. They wouldn't name him Lycurgus Ezekiel Savage after his grandfather.

A letter from Papa brought the news that the baby was to be Clay Savage, Junior. He was to receive the name officially next week when Father O'Connell would come to baptize him.

"He is the very image of me," wrote Papa, in the beautiful shaded letters Luvvy found so hard to make in penmanship class.

But he made no mention of the Girls coming home for the baptism. He did write that Mama would be in bed for a couple of weeks, so they wouldn't be driving to Frederick very soon.

The Little Girls were beginning to tire of hearing about the baby.

"After all," Eunice told Luvvy, "lots of the girls here have brothers."

They couldn't understand that little Clay was a special kind of brother. Even Agatha, who had been so interested, was avoiding her. She would sit by herself in the playroom busily crocheting.

"Will you teach me how?" asked Luvvy, watching the needle twitching so rapidly and surely.

"Not now," said Agatha impatiently. "I'm busy making this doily for Auntie Sister."

When Papa did bring Mama and the baby to Frederick, it was early spring and the snow was gone. Regina and Marylou didn't come with them because the little girl had a cold and they didn't want her to get close to the baby.

Papa didn't smoke in the parlor because he was afraid it wouldn't be good for such a young baby. Mama held the pink bundle tenderly.

"Can I hold him for awhile, Mama?" begged Luvvy. "Please! Please!"

Mama was very particular. "Get seated in this chair first. There! Now support the back of his head with one hand. Don't squeeze him too hard."

Luvvy looked down at the wizened little face that looked old enough to belong to Lycurgus Ezekiel. The baby clenched his tiny fists, kicked his legs, and made mouths at her.

"His eyes are blue like Hetty's and Marylou's," Luvvy noted.

"They may turn brown," warned Mama. "Babies are often born with blue eyes that darken in time."

"What will he be when he grows up?" asked Luvvy.

"Rich man, poor man, beggar man, thief, soldier,

sailor, merchant, chief," quoted Betsey.

"He'll be a rich man like Papa," Luvvy guessed.

"Whoa, there!" exclaimed Papa. "I'm not as rich as you girls seem to think when you go shopping."

"I do wish that war in Europe would end," said Mama in a worried voice. "I certainly don't want him to be a soldier."

"Everybody was stirred up about the sinking of the *Lusitania*," said Papa, "but all that has died down now. I didn't vote for Wilson, but I think he has done a good job of keeping us out of the war."

"I certainly don't want Alec to have to go to war," put in Hetty.

Europe and the war. So far away from Maryland. So far away from Alec and little Clay.

"Perhaps he'll be a lawyer," suggested Luvvy, "since that's what you wanted Regina to be."

"A lawyer or a doctor," Papa decided. He winked at Luvvy. "And if he wants to run for governor of Maryland, I won't stand in his way."

There was a discreet knock on the parlor door, and Sister Veronica entered. Since she had already admired the baby, she stated her mission.

"I have a little gift here from my great-niece Agatha," she said. "It's a cap for the dear little baby. She crocheted it all by herself."

Luvvy was the first to take it from her hand. "So that's why she didn't want me around when she was

94

crocheting," she said. "But why didn't she bring it herself? I want her to see the baby."

"She didn't want to intrude in a family meeting," explained Sister Veronica. "Oh, dear! I hope it fits."

"Please try to find Agatha, Sister, and bring her in," said Luvvy. "I want Papa and Mama to meet her."

A few minutes later the door swung open and Agatha timidly entered.

Luvvy hurried to her and took her hand.

"Papa and Mama, this is Agatha."

"The little girl who lives at the convent," Mama remembered. "Thank you so much for your thoughtful gift. You do beautiful work."

Luvvy added her thanks. "You surely fooled me about the crocheting," she admitted. "A doily for Sister Veronica!"

Agatha clasped her hands and stared at little Clay with a lonely look of admiration.

"He looks just like a baby doll," she said. "I'm so happy you have him. Luvvy hasn't been able to talk about anything else."

"I can hardly wait until I get home Easter to play with him all day long," declared Luvvy.

9.
The Invitation

By March the eighth grade was studying poetry.

"How many kinds of verse do we have in English?" asked Sister Mary Clare.

"Four," parroted Luvvy. "Iambic, trochaic, ana-pestic, and dactylic." It had taken her almost half an hour to memorize such hard words.

Questions went on to other girls.

Luvvy yawned and looked out of the window. The trees were in bud again. The grass in the plots was turning green. It was hard to remember the puffy white comforter of snow that had covered the yard not too long ago.

"Rhetorical beauty in versification requires that the subject of discourse be of an agreeable nature," Sister Mary Clare's voice droned on.

Luvvy wished Sister would begin reading some poetry instead of talking about it. She liked ballads best of all because they told a story, usually tragic. Her favorite poem was "The Arab's Farewell to His Steed." She had learned it by heart. Perhaps she would have a chance to recite it that afternoon. Miss Font le Roy came from town on Friday afternoons to teach them dramatic art, etiquette, and physical culture.

Limericks were interesting too. It was easy to write a funny limerick. You didn't have to be Milton or Shakespeare. She had one running around in her head.

Luvvy began to write it down. Then she tore that part of the page from her tablet and crushed it into a little ball. She tried to catch Agatha's eye.

"Ps's'st! Ps's'st!"

Agatha's desk wasn't far away. She looked around.

Sister Mary Clare's eye caught the paper ball when Agatha's hand fumbled it.

"Bring that to my desk, Agatha," she sternly ordered.

Agatha gave Luvvy an apologetic look, then obeyed. Sister flattened out the paper on her desk and quickly read it to herself.

"I shall share this with the class," she announced. She read:

> There was a good nun of Frederick
> Who taught composition and rhetoric.
> She said, "It is me
> Is illiteracy,"
> That rhetorical nun of Frederick.

Titters went through the classroom.

"Will the author of this versification please stand up," demanded Sister.

Luvvy rose with bowed head. She was humiliated and worried. Now Sister Mary Clare wouldn't like her anymore. She was very fond of her teacher, so she really wasn't making fun of her. It was only a limerick.

"It is a very good limerick, Luvena," said Sister. She paused while Luvvy gained heart. "It's so good that I'm going to ask you to remain after class while the others are at recess and write twenty-five copies of it for me. But first, look up the meaning of 'illiteracy' in the dictionary. You, Agatha, may remain with Luvena and study iambic verse."

Luvvy flopped into her seat dejectedly. Now that the weather was warming, it was so much fun to play outside again.

She hoped things would go better in Miss Font le

Roy's class. It was held in the big music room where there was a stage with a grand piano and two harps. Rows of chairs filled the room when there were plays or concerts, and it was the scene of Commencement Day exercises.

When Luvvy entered the room, there were some Big Girls practicing with dumbbells. They raised and lowered them rhythmically. Betsey, who was among them, was clowning. She acted as if the dumbbells were great weights that could scarcely be lifted.

Miss Font le Roy came sweeping in like the leading lady in a play. She was a tall, dark-haired woman in a black suit. "So stylish-looking," Hetty always described her.

When she signaled for class to begin, Luvvy hoped she would start with the recitations.

"Today, girls," said Miss Font le Roy, speaking from her diaphragm in pear-shaped tones, "we are going to learn to faint gracefully."

Although somewhat disappointed, Luvvy was interested. This sounded like something different. But if you fainted, you were unconscious. And if you were unconscious, how would you know if you were fainting gracefully?

Miss Font le Roy gave a demonstration. "Don't fall like a stick," she warned. "Slowly collapse from your feet up so you fall to the floor as gracefully as a silken ribbon." She began slumping, then gracefully sank to the floor with arms flung out. "You see what I mean," she said, gracefully rising. "Now we will begin with Hester Savage."

Luvvy was proud of Hetty. She fainted as gracefully as her teacher. As her back touched the floor, she turned slightly so that her face was up and her arms formed a half circle.

"She looks just like a picture I saw of a Christian martyr," Luvvy whispered to Agatha.

One Big Girl after another fainted, gracefully or awkwardly.

"Now, Luvena," beckoned Miss Font le Roy. "Let us see how well the Little Girls can do."

Luvvy took the center of the stage. She closed her eyes and tried to imagine herself a silken ribbon. She bent her knees and thumped to the floor. There was a numbness in her elbow when she hit her "crazy bone."

Miss Font le Roy helped her up.

"You will have to practice more, Luvena," she said. "And your skirt went up above your knees. You will never want that to happen if you ever really faint in public."

The girls found the fainting great fun. They kept practicing it in the playroom that evening.

Mary Leary had an interesting bit of information.

"I heard that putting wet blotters inside your shoes

will make you faint," she told Betsey. "It draws the blood from your head."

Betsey was enthusiastic. "I'm going to bring some up to my curtain tonight, and try it out tomorrow morning so I can faint in chapel."

"Oh, please don't," Luvvy implored her.

The idea of Betsey really fainting frightened her.

Her entreaties had no effect. Betsey smuggled the blotters up to the dormitory. They were hidden in her drawer all night.

Next morning Luvvy peeped into her curtain to see Betsey dipping the blotters into the water pitcher. She fitted them inside her high shoes.

"Ugh!" she complained at sight of Luvvy. "It feels like I'm walking in slush."

"Please don't faint in chapel," Luvvy again implored her.

The girls soon lined up with their black veils on their heads. They tramped out of the dormitory onto the porch. As the line made a hairpin turn down the outside stairs, Luvvy could see that Betsey limped slightly because her shoes were too tight.

All through Mass, Luvvy cast apprehensive glances back to Betsey until Sister Mary Rose tapped her on the shoulder and ordered her to read her missal.

Was Betsey getting pale? Would she really faint? If she did, there would be a commotion in back, and then Luvvy would feel free to turn around.

Betsey didn't faint. She was quite well all that day. It was the day after that she began sniffling and complaining that her ears hurt.

Sister Mary Anne gave her medicine, but the cold got worse so Betsey was put to bed up in the infirmary.

"Will you bring these books up to your sister?" Betsey's teacher asked Luvvy soon after. "I don't want her to fall behind in her work."

Luvvy dutifully carried the books up to the infirmary. Betsey was propped up on pillows with a mound of handkerchiefs at hand. Her eyes were watery and her nose looked like a rosebud.

She was glad to see Luvvy, but not the books. "I wish I had left those blotters alone," she repented in a hoarse voice. "I might have known they wouldn't work."

"They gave you a cold," said Luvvy. "You look awful."

"A cold isn't as graceful as fainting."

Luvvy looked around the room, as it was her first visit. There were beds and chairs, a table, and a stove built into the wall.

"That's a funny kind of stove," said Luvvy. "I've never seen one like it before."

"It's a Latrobe heater," said Betsey. "It heats the room up above too. See the hot-air registers in the side? They connect with others up above."

103

"What's up there?"

"It's the room for anybody with contagious sick-
ness so nobody else will catch it. Hetty and I were
quarantined up there when we had the measles last
Easter. We had fun talking through the registers to
any girls who were below."

This intrigued Luvvy. She went over to the stove
and called "Hello" through the grating.

"There's nobody up there now, thank goodness,"
said Betsey.

The spring days grew warmer as the weeks passed
by.

One Saturday, Sister Mary Cecilia told the girls,
"Those of you who wash your hair today may dry it
on the upper porch."

The girls washed their hair in the bathroom with its
tubs and basins. They then climbed the steps to the
highest porch where the warm breeze was strongest.

It was a lazy, pleasant feeling to sit in the sunshine
with the hair hanging over their faces and let the
breeze fan it.

"It takes forever to dry my hair because it's so long
and thick," said Luvvy. "But I don't care because
it's nice to sit up here and look down on the yard.
As if we're up in a balloon."

"You don't know what a nuisance it is when hair's
as curly as mine," complained Eunice. "I can hardly

get the comb through it afterward, it snarls so." She was really very proud of her hair, which gave off coppery glints in the sunshine. She wound tendrils around her forefinger then flicked them loose.

"Why don't you cut it off," said Agatha mischievously. She knew Eunice's pet vanity.

"Then you could be a nun," suggested Luvvy. That was the thing that distressed her most about Regina's going into the convent.

They laughed and chatted gaily, rubbing their heads with the towels and then flinging their hair to the breeze.

Luvvy moved her chair closer to the railing and let her black mop hang over it.

"My hair hung down like this when I used to perform on the trapeze," she said, "but it was in braids so I could see."

"You really can perform on a trapeze?" asked Eunice in awe.

"Papa taught me to hang by my knees. He always did like circuses. It was great fun. I'd start the trapeze swinging, then let go of the ropes and let myself fall backward."

"Can you still do it?" asked Agatha.

A daring idea came to Luvvy.

"Want to see me hang by my knees from this railing?"

"Oh, no, no!" cried Agatha.

Luvvy paid no attention. She tossed her hair back and sat on the railing facing them. She slowly arched her back and dropped down until the insides of her knees clung to the railing.

Eunice shrieked and Agatha grabbed a leg.

"It's all right," called Luvvy. The blood ran to her head and her long hair floated below.

Seeing the convent grounds upside down was a peculiar sight.

The girls below looked like flies on a parquet ceiling. The nuns in the monastery grounds were slow-moving beetles. Trees seemed to hang down like green Christmas ornaments. Her floor was the wide blue sky carpeted by a few sheepskin clouds.

There was a sudden commotion among the flies. They began scurrying about madly, then gathered in a cluster. A beetle was flying to the upside-down staircase with black wings spread.

By the time Luvvy pulled herself back to the railing and slid off, Sister Mary Cecilia came bursting out of the door.

"What happened?" she cried breathlessly. "Who nearly fell off the porch?"

"I was hanging by my knees, Sister," admitted Luvvy.

"How did you lose your balance?" panted Sister. "You've been told to stay back from the railing."

"I didn't lose my balance. I was showing the girls how I used to hang from a trapeze."

"You mean you did it on *purpose?*"

"Yes, Sister."

Sister Mary Cecilia let out an explosive breath. Her eyes flashed with indignation.

"Then you'll come with me to Mother Mary Austin's office immediately," she commanded.

Now aware of the enormity of her crime, Luvvy followed the nun's black habit. She silently followed her down all the stairways and into the hall.

Mother Mary Austin's office had been General McClellan's headquarters during the Union occupation of Frederick.

As Sister Mary Cecilia brought her charges, Luvvy thought that Mother Mary Austin had never looked more like a stern Union general. So must many a soldier have quaked in his boots standing here under like circumstances.

Luvvy waited to be expelled from the Visitation Academy.

"Such a reckless act is almost unbelievable," said the Reverend Mother. "And to think it was committed by a student whose family has attended this school for three generations." Of course Grandma Savage and Aunt Molly never would have done such a thing. They had never learned to perform on a trapeze. "And with an older sister who is going to become a nun. And another who won the deportment medal last year."

Luvvy had once yearned to earn that medal herself, but had soon lost interest because of the temptations of boarding-school life.

She stood with damp, bowed head, waiting to be sentenced.

"Think of what would have happened if you had fallen," continued Mother Mary Austin. "No parents would ever have entrusted their daughter to our care again. Your own never would have forgiven us. Promise me that you will never do such a thing in the future."

Then she wasn't going to be expelled after all. She solemnly made the promise.

"Now I want you to sit on the penance bench for an hour and consider the seriousness of your prank."

"Yes, Reverend Mother. Thank you, Reverend Mother."

Luvvy was glad to get away even if it meant an hour of penance. She finished drying her hair on the outside bench. She thought of what would have happened if she had fallen. She remembered the funeral of Maudie, her little sister, and how it had affected everyone in the family.

As the story traveled around, girls would come and stare at her a few moments with curiosity or admiration. She would henceforth share fame with the girl who went up on the rope with her trunk.

Agatha kept hovering a few yards away now that her own wispy hair was dry. She cast sympathetic glances at Luvvy.

When the hour was up and Luvvy had been excused from the bench, she was surrounded by the Little Girls.

"I'm shocked that you tried to commit suicide after all," said Amy who had not washed her own hair that Saturday. "I thought you were only joking that first day I met you."

"She wasn't trying to commit suicide," declared Agatha. "She was showing us how she can hang from a trapeze."

"That was wicked too," declared Amy. "I'm ashamed that a friend of mine would do such a thing."

The worst was the scolding she received from her sisters.

"You know I'm responsible for you, Luvvy," said Hetty. "Papa and Mama Della will think that I've failed in taking care of you properly."

"Now the nuns won't let us dry our hair up on that porch anymore," said Betsey.

Luvvy wished she had never washed her hair that day.

Agatha was the only one who seemed to understand. "You really shouldn't have done it, Luvvy," she reasoned, "but I know how easily it happened with us talking about the trapeze."

"I know I shouldn't have," admitted Luvvy. "Now I won't have any peace from the girls or the nuns until Easter vacation."

"It's not far off," said Agatha. "The girls will forget all about it during the holidays. And I'll be here to help the nuns think about other things."

Luvvy stared at Agatha as if she had just met her. Why hadn't she thought of this before?

"Agatha, would you like to come home with me for Easter?" she invited.

The other girl stared at her with amazement and disbelief. She seemed to have lost her tongue.

"I know it will be all right with Mama," Luvvy went on quickly. "You've met her and Papa, and they liked you. I'll write home right away. The Girls can always bring anyone they want to visit."

"Do you really mean it?" asked Agatha. "Really?"

"Of course, or I wouldn't ask you. I may hang by my knees from a porch, but I don't tease my best friend."

"I'd love to, Luvvy. I really, really would. I'll run and tell Auntie Sister right away. I know she'll let me go."

10.

Easter

The Girls were bubbling with excitement as they waited for Papa to arrive in the Machine to take them home for Easter. Much earlier than necessary, they had piled their suitcases in the front hall. Agatha's imitation leather one looked brand new because it had traveled so little.

Some of the girls, including Mary Letitia, had already left, and others would have to wait another day. Those lugging their heavy suitcases down the stairs were the envy of the ones left behind, even if only for a day.

"I just can't believe I'm really going with you," Agatha kept saying over and over to Luvvy.

111

"We'll ride horseback and play games and wheel little Clay around," Luvvy promised.

When Sister Veronica finally opened the door to Papa, the Girls nearly bowled him over with their affectionate assault.

"We'll help you carry our suitcases out," offered Betsey, who had grabbed her own after hugging and kissing him.

"It's so kind of you and dear Mrs. Savage to offer your hospitality to my dear little niece," said Sister Veronica to Papa. "You may find her a lively child, but Agatha really has a deeply religious nature."

Luvvy and Agatha giggled.

At last the suitcases had been strapped to the back of the Machine. It was a big town model with two little seats that pulled out in back, but they didn't need to use them since only Papa had come. Hetty sat in front with him, and the others on the back seat.

Agatha hardly took her eyes from the scenery that passed by. It was as if she herself were a nun who was returning to the world.

Once through Knoxville, they crossed the Baltimore & Ohio tracks twice. Then they were on the last lap of the trip where the road ran through the ravine.

Agatha was overawed at her first view of Shady Grove. It was a large stone house with two white frame wings. An upper and lower porch with lacy white banisters fitted between the wings. It was almost hidden by the grove of old shade trees.

"It's beautiful!" exclaimed Agatha. "Which floor do you live on?"

The Girls laughed.

"We live on all of them," said Luvvy, "and sometimes they don't seem enough."

Agatha was even more impressed. "When I was little, we lived in a tenement building almost that big, but we only had the upper floor."

When Papa let them out at the gate, they raced up the brick walk. Marylou was waiting for them with her finger in her mouth.

"Why didn't you come sooner?" she asked as they embraced her in turn. "Who is this new girl? Is she my sister?"

"Almost," said Luvvy. "She's my best friend. And Agatha, this can't be anybody but Marylou."

They hurried inside to see the others. They were most eager to see little Clay, but he came last because he was asleep upstairs.

"I remember Agatha from last year," said Regina. "You were in seventh grade then. Hetty, I'm going to move back into our old room with you and Betsey so the two girls can have my bedroom. We set up a cot in it for Luvvy. I think girl friends like to talk privately before they fall asleep."

That evening was festive because Alec drove from Brunswick in his buggy to welcome Hetty home. He brought a big box of chocolates with him. Luvvy thought they were as good as the Misses Beckley's operas. Later they all gathered around the piano to sing popular songs.

That night as the two Little Girls lay in bed reliving the day, Agatha said, "I think Alec is handsome. He's so romantic."

"Hetty's romantic too," said Luvvy.

"Do you want to get married when you grow up?"

Luvvy sighed. "I guess I'll have to if I want to write about married people. I wrote a story about them once, and it was so silly I threw it away."

Agatha soon felt at home at Shady Grove. She and Luvvy took turns wheeling Clay around until they tired of him.

"He'll be more fun when he gets older and can do things," Luvvy decided.

She took Agatha for long horseback rides. She sat in the saddle with Agatha behind, clinging to her waist as Maudie had done. They rode to the blockhouses on the canal where the poor squatters lived, and to the Harpers Ferry bridge, and once all the way to Brunswick to buy a thermometer for Mama.

Waiting for Easter had always dragged so, but with Agatha time went fast. They hardly realized it was Easter eve until they saw Pansy carrying a basket of eggs into the kitchen.

"You and Agatha may dye the eggs for the Children if you wish," said Mama to Luvvy.

That evening she dissolved packets of different colors into small dishes for them. Martha, the cook, watched with a stern eye to see that they didn't spill anything on her clean linoleum floor.

When the colored eggs had dried, the girls arranged them in baskets Mama had bought at the notion store in Brunswick. They looked like a king's jewels. Great nuggets of ruby and jade and sapphire and topaz. Maybe a king's ransom.

After Marylou had gone to sleep, one was set at the foot of her bed. The other was put next to little Clay's cradle. At least he could look at them next day.

Marylou wasn't the only one who was surprised Easter morning. When Luvvy and Agatha woke up, they saw two strange new dresses laid over the backs of the chairs. One was striped pink and the other blue Both had puffy white organdy sashes. And on the bureau were two straw hats, one trimmed with artificial daisies, the other with red cherries.

The girls jumped out of bed and stared at them.

"We must have slept soundly," said Luvvy. "These are our Easter presents, I'm sure. Mama always makes me a new dress for Easter. The pink one would look prettiest on you," she added. "And the hat with daisies would go best with that."

115

Agatha's dress was a little big because Mama hadn't known her exact size. "But it looks all right for now," said Luvvy, "and Mama can take it in later."

Agatha stared at the girl in the mirror as if she were an elegant stranger.

"I look downright nobby," she declared.

Both girls were quite dwarfed by the profusion of flowers on the hats that had been bought at the Misses Higgins' millinery shop in Harpers Ferry.

After the ride in the Machine to Mass in St. Francis of Assisi Church in Brunswick, Luvvy saddled Valley and Dolly.

"You can ride Dolly, and I'll take Valley because she's skittish," Luvvy told Agatha. "We'll just walk the horses today until you get used to sitting in the saddle."

Next day they did a little trotting. "You rise up and down in the stirrups like this in time to the gait," Luvvy demonstrated. "It's called posting to the trot. Then you won't get shaken up. When you canter, just relax and sway with the saddle as if you're in a rocking chair."

Sometimes Agatha posted, but other times the horse shook her like cream in a butter churn.

When they tired of horseback riding and playing with Clay, they took walks through the fields or down the roads.

"Let's walk to Weverton today and watch the

Baltimore express go through," suggested Luvvy one day. "We can wave to the engineer."

Arm in arm they went down the dirt road toward the little village. As they entered the ravine, they saw two girls who looked about their age walking ahead.

Luvvy had often seen them go past her house. One had hair twisted back from her temples and hanging in long braids like her own. The other had bound her braids around her head as Betsey sometimes did.

"Let's catch up with them," suggested Agatha quickening her steps.

"I don't know them," said Luvvy hesitantly. Then she added "But I'd like to."

Somehow she had never been interested in who the girls were. She supposed that they lived in Sandy Hook. But now Agatha made getting acquainted with them seem like an adventure.

"Hello!" called Agatha. "Wait for us!"

The girls looked around in surprise then stopped. Agatha and Luvvy hurried to them.

"Want to walk with us?" invited Agatha. "We're going to watch the express go by."

"I'm Luvvy Savage and she's Agatha Mulcahy," said Luvvy. "I live at Shady Grove, and she's visiting me."

"Yes, we know," said the girl with braids hanging. "I'm Dixie Tompkins and this is my sister Nellie."

Luvvy found it so much easier to talk to strange

girls now that she had been at Frederick. She didn't feel tongue-tied and shy as she had that first day at the convent.

"Where are you going?" she asked.

"We're on our way to see Uncle Pat and Aunt Ida. Their canal boat will be going through the Weverton lock this afternoon."

"It's due, anyway," said Nellie. "Uncle Pat is captain of Number 29."

Luvvy had lived near the Chesapeake & Ohio Canal for most of her childhood. She had enjoyed watching the little boats go through the lock, too. They plied the canal between Cumberland and the District of Columbia, carrying coal from the mines in western Maryland. How interesting it must be to have a relative on one!

"My older sister once had a picnic on a canal boat," said Luvvy. "They ate their lunches on deck, then got off at the Harpers Ferry lock."

"We're going to ride there on Uncle Pat's boat," said Dixie. "He's on his way back to Cumberland."

"Last summer a circus horse Papa had bought near Hagerstown was brought here on a boat," Luvvy added.

"I remember when the horse got loose and was hit by a train," said Nellie. "That was too bad."

It was strange that these girls knew more about her affairs than she did about theirs.

"Pepper was my special pet," she said. "It just broke my heart."

"Yes, I saw you with him on your lawn one time," said Dixie. "You were standing on his back."

"You did? I used to think I wanted to be a bare-back rider in a circus. I guess you live in Sandy Hook."

"Yes, Pa is a brakeman on the railroad," said Nellie.

"My father rides the train to Hagerstown and back almost every day."

"I know," said Dixie. "He has a tool factory there."

They went across the stone bridge at the bottom of the ravine then crossed the railroad tracks.

"Why don't you come with us to see Uncle Pat's boat?" invited Dixie.

"We'd love to," Luvvy accepted. "That will be more interesting than watching an old train go by."

They crossed the sluiceway bridge by the lock-tender's little stone house and went on to the lock. Two sets of gates trapped water which could be raised or lowered to the water levels on either side of the lock. It was like a stairstep for boats. Across was the towpath for the mules. It was bordered by trees that screened the rock-strewn waters of the Potomac River.

The girls sat in the grass on the bank waiting for Number 29.

"Maybe you'd like to go with us on the ride to the Harpers Ferry lock," invited Dixie.

Luvvy clapped her hands with childish enthusiasm. "Oh, thank you. All my life I've wanted to ride on a canal boat, but I never had the chance. I was broken-hearted when the Big Girls wouldn't take me on the picnic with them. I have three older sisters, you know."

"Yes," said Dixie. "They're by your father's first marriage."

"Do you have any sisters or brothers?" asked Luvvy.

"No," said Dixie. "Just us. Some people think we're twins but we're really a year apart. I'm thirteen and Nellie's twelve."

"I'm thirteen too," said Agatha.

"I'm three-quarters past twelve, and a quarter to thirteen by railroad time," Luvvy joked because she felt so at ease with the girls.

Their laughter was cut short when Dixie suddenly jumped up.

"Look! There's a boat coming."

All the girls got up and walked closer to the lock. They shaded their eyes as they tried to see the boat better.

Nellie began jumping up and down. "It's Mutt and Jeff, and Pete driving them," she cried.

Slowly the tandem of mules approached. A long rope stretching behind them was tied to the blunt prow of Number 29.

"It looks like a Noah's ark," declared Agatha.

"Specially with those two mules looking out of those little curved windows in front," said Luvvy.

"That's the stable," explained Dixie. "One team rests and eats while the other works."

"Hi, Pete," called Dixie.

The towpath boy waved his frayed straw hat to them. He drove the mules on past the lock gate. Since the water in it was already low, the boat could be maneuvered in right away.

"That's Skip, the helmsman, pushing with the boat pole," explained Nellie. "Hello, Skip."

Uncle Pat, a bearded man with a visored cap set jauntily over his bushy eyebrows, waved to them. Behind him at the stern were his living quarters, covered by an awning. Tiny windows were decorated with checked red and white curtains. Red geraniums bloomed in miniature window boxes below them.

Aunt Ida called greetings from the entryway. She was almost as fat as the Misses Beckley, but her expression was more cheery.

The girls looked down at the wet moss-grown rock walls of the lock. Number 29 was down deep. The gates were closed behind it. Water began flowing in from the upstream gates as they slowly opened. As the water rose, so did the boat. When it was only a few feet below them, Dixie and Nellie jumped down on deck.

121

"Come on," they called to Luvvy and Agatha.

The other girls hesitated long enough for the boat to come higher, then hopped down.

"They're Luvvy Savage and Agatha Mulcahy," Dixie introduced them. "You know the Savages live in that big old farmhouse up the road. They can ride to Harpers Ferry, can't they?"

"Sure thing," said Uncle Pat. "Always need a bigger crew. Now which of you will drive the mules and which handle the tiller?"

Uncle Pat reminded Luvvy of Papa.

The gates ahead were fully open and Number 29 was on the upper canal level. But there was more work to be done. Mutt and Jeff were unhitched from the tow line to trade places with the other team. A big fallboard was laid to get the mules between bank and boat.

They were soon on their way again. The boat glided lazily up the canal past heavily wooded foothills and rocky outcroppings that pushed against railroad tracks.

"Want to see down below, where they live?" asked Nellie.

Luvvy and Agatha followed her down the entryway steps into what seemed like the underground abode of dwarfs. A tiny kitchen with a table no bigger than a Parcheesi board. A little stove whose entire top was covered by the pot of simmering chicken stew.

The two little staterooms with regular-sized bunk beds.

"It must be fun to keep house here," said Luvvy. "It would be like playing house."

"You always have a changing view from the windows," said Nellie.

The girls then went up on deck and sat on the roof of the center cabin.

"The feed and hay for the mules is stowed here," said Dixie.

"But where do they carry the cargo?" asked Agatha.

"Under the deck," explained Dixie. "It's empty now. That's why the boat is riding so high. But it will be full of coal on the return trip."

Luvvy leaned back. "I feel like Cleopatra floating down the Nile," she said languorously.

Sandy Hook came into view.

"There's our house," cried Dixie, pointing to a white cottage clinging to the mountainside.

"I'm glad to know where it is," said Luvvy. "Now I'll know where to find you."

The long string of cottages unrolled against the high mountain.

There was a roar from the tunnel that pierced the rocky cliff. The black snout of an engine sprang from the dark hole and charged down the track.

"The Baltimore express!" cried Luvvy.

It coiled around the green curves, its whistle warning the crossings ahead. The girls waved wildly. Uncle Pat waved a clenched fist.

"Durned rascal!" he shouted. "Trying to take away my business."

"But Pa works on the railroad," protested Dixie.

"He ought to be at the tiller of this boat," said Uncle Pat.

Number 29 passed under the Harpers Ferry bridge where the Shenandoah flowed into the Potomac. At last the plodding mules reached the lock.

"I wish we could go all the way to Cumberland," said Luvvy.

"I reckon you'd get tired of it after awhile," said Skip. "Specially if you had to mind the tiller or walk behind the mules."

The long walk home seemed as endless as the towpath. It seemed even longer when the Tompkins girls left them in Sandy Hook.

"You'll come to Shady Grove tomorrow, won't you?" Luvvy invited them. "We can play Parcheesi or something."

"We'd like anything you want to do," said Dixie. "I've always wondered what it was like inside your house."

Luvvy and Agatha finally reached the orchards above the vegetable garden.

"To think they've always been here and I've never

known them before!" exclaimed Luvvy. "Think of all the years of fun I've missed by not having them to play with."

11.

Violets

Back at the convent, the girls soon fell into school routine again. They now looked forward to the Saturday walks into town. After one of these, Mabel Courtney came running to where some of them were sitting under the twin elms.

"We're going out again tomorrow afternoon," she announced. "I heard Sister Mary Rose talking to some of the Big Girls about it."

"Where? Where?" was the breathless question.

Luvvy was particularly anxious to know. After the carefree Easter vacation, the convent walls were beginning to tighten around her again. The trip to town had been tantalizing enough to make her wish for yet another outing.

"Guess where?" teased Mabel.

"The Deaf School to watch them play mumblety-peg?" asked Eunice. "We did that last year. Remember how we tried to learn their sign language so we could talk back and forth in the study room?"

Mabel shook her head.

"To the Jug Bridge?" asked Agatha. "I've been there so often already."

Mabel couldn't hold the important information back any longer.

"The cemetery," she said. "We're going to the cemetery."

Luvvy was disappointed.

"Did somebody die?" she asked.

"No, silly. We're going there to pick violets."

Amy spoke words that could have come straight from *Agnes of the Lilies*. "And it will make us think more seriously about the hereafter."

To Luvvy's surprise the other girls were filled with delight.

"I might have known," said Eunice. "We always take a walk there in the spring. I've never seen such gorgeous violets anywhere else. You think about the hereafter, Amy, while we pick them."

"We have a lot of violets growing in our yard at home," said Luvvy. She couldn't imagine anyone being thrilled over the prospect of going to a cemetery to pick them. The woods, maybe, or even a field.

Agatha sensed her disappointment. "It's really a beautiful place," she assured Luvvy. "There's a monument there to Francis Scott Key—and Barbara Fritchie too."

Luvvy brooded over the forthcoming outing. Now that she knew Agatha so well, she felt free to open her heart to her.

"I don't know if I want to go on that walk to the cemetery," she said. "It makes me feel sad even to think about it. The last time I went to one was when they buried my little sister Maudie."

Agatha's thin face grew even more pointed with compassion. She reached for Luvvy's hand.

"I know," she sympathized. "Mama and Papa were both buried at the same time."

"What happened to them?" asked Luvvy. She had never felt free to ask such a personal question before.

"I've never talked to anybody else much about it, but it was when our tenement caught on fire. The firemen got me out but—" Her voice choked and she wasn't able to finish.

Luvvy squeezed her hand.

"I'm real sorry."

Agatha quickly gained control of herself. "But now that I've gone on the outings to the cemetery every spring, I don't feel so bad about it. There are so many people that have died. And lots of soldiers."

Luvvy nodded. "There are Confederate soldiers in

Maudie's cemetery too. She used to love stories so much that I imagine them all gathered around her telling about bivouacs and cavalry charges—like old Mr. Johnson in Harpers Ferry."

Now that they had spoken of their sorrows to each other, they felt relieved. As if sharing grief was as important as sharing the happy times they had had during Easter vacation.

"The violets there really are beautiful," said Agatha. "We fill vases for the shrines and our tables. And you should see the big Francis Scott Key monument. People come from all around to look at it."

Luvvy found herself really excited about the excursion.

They set out again as they had the day before. A long line of girls in twos, with a nun ahead and one behind. This time Sister Veronica and Sister Mary Rose carried empty baskets.

They turned the corner between the convent and St. John's Church, following narrow Chapel Street to East Patrick.

"Barbara Fritchie's house is down this street," said Agatha.

"Will we get to see it?" asked Luvvy.

"We turn off before we get there."

"Let's ask Sister Mary Rose if we can go past it," suggested Luvvy.

She and Agatha ran to the head of the line.

"Please, Sister," panted Agatha, "may we go past the Barbara Fritchie house so Luvvy can see it?"

Some of the Big Girls groaned.

"It's out of the way."

"And such a long walk to the cemetery anyway."

Sister Mary Rose sided with the two Little Girls.

"It will be cultural and rewarding," she said. "We shall go down West Patrick, then swing around on South Street. The exercise is good for you."

"But we've seen it before," complained a tall lanky girl whom Luvvy recognized as one of Hetty's friends.

"A worthwhile sight is worth seeing more than once," pronounced Sister. "If you saw the Sistine Chapel once, you'd be willing to see it again."

So, like Stonewall Jackson's men, they marched past the little brick house with its sloping roof and high dormer windows. Luvvy could almost see Dame Fritchie's face framed by a ruffled white bonnet at the window.

She kept turning her head to look at the house as they passed. She stumbled over the uneven brick sidewalk, and would have fallen if Agatha hadn't grabbed her arm.

This sidetrip into history did make the walk much longer. It seemed to the girls that "All day long through Frederick street, Sounded the tread of marching feet."

At last, hot and tired, they reached the shady green cemetery with its white headstones. Some of the girls flung themselves on the grass to rest. Others began wandering down the winding paths. The Big Girls were putting as many tombstones between themselves and the nuns as possible.

Luvvy and Agatha stopped to stare at the imposing Francis Scott Key monument near the entrance. It dominated the cemetery. The figure of the patriotic songwriter stood on top of a round column. His arms were flung upward and one hand held a sheaf of papers.

"He looks so real," said Agatha in a half-whisper as if they were in church. "That must be 'The Star Spangled Banner' in his hand. He's probably just finished writing it."

"I don't think so," said Luvvy critically. "I think he's standing on the deck of the British ship and looking through the dawn's early light at those broad stripes and bright stars still flying. I couldn't write a poem with all that going on around me."

They found a clump of violets nearby, then went on down one of the walks. From time to time, they left the path to gather more flowers.

Luvvy held one up by its delicate stem. "It does look shy, doesn't it?" she asked. "See how it hangs its head. My oldest sister Regina has a party gown this color. She's going to give it to me when she goes to the convent. But I won't be able to wear it until I grow up."

"Are you going to be shy and hang your head at parties?"

They laughed as if it were a great joke.

"Here are some more shy ones hiding under this tree," directed Luvvy.

"Look at those near that gravestone," said Agatha. "They have such long stems."

"Over there! They're even prettier. They look like tiny purple butterflies perched among the leaves."

They found some little gray Confederate violets near an oak. A red squirrel ran up the tree and shrilly scolded the girls as they crouched below. Luvvy laughed and threw a violet up at him.

Now and then they stopped their search in order to look at tombstones and read the inscriptions. A great iron anchor was propped against a gray stone. They tiptoed across the grass to it.

"It's Captain Ordeman and he died in 1884," said Agatha.

"He must have been in the Navy because of that anchor," reasoned Luvvy. "I bet he was in the Civil War."

They turned to a nearby tombstone surmounted by the plaque of a clipper ship with its many masts and sails.

"It's John Ordeman and he died in 1875," Luvvy

read. "He was Captain Ordeman's father, and he ran away to Baltimore when he was only a boy. Then he joined the crew of a fast clipper and sailed around the world. But he never forgot his childhood sweetheart in Frederick. So one day when he was grown up and rich, he came back here and married her."

"How do you know?" asked Agatha. "It doesn't say all that on the tombstone."

"I think it must have been that way. So they settled down here, and soon a baby boy was born to them."

"Go on," urged Agatha. "I like to listen to your stories."

"The little boy was like you and Maudie. He loved to listen to his father's stories about the clipper ships and foreign lands. So when he grew up, he went to sea too. Then the Civil War began and he joined the Confederate Navy. He was on the *Merrimac* when it fought the *Monitor*. Although he knew that it was hopeless, he kept shooting off his cannon for two whole days and a night. Even when he was badly wounded, he stayed at his post. He was so brave that he was promoted to captain and given his own ship."

"Then what happened?"

"I don't know. I'll have to think about it for awhile. He must have come back to Frederick since he's buried here."

"But there aren't any Ordeman women's names on

these tombstones," said Agatha. "What happened to their wives?"

Luvvy quickly provided for them. "John Ordeman's wife went on a voyage with him one time, but she fell overboard off the China coast during a storm and was lost at sea. And Captain Ordeman never married because the woman he loved married another man when he was at the war, so he never wanted to have anything more to do with women."

They picked more violets, carrying the mass of them in their uplifted skirts. They rested on the grass for a short while. Luvvy separated a small bouquet from her trove and pulled the stems through a buttonhole of Agatha's sweater. She twined some of them through her own long braids.

As they went down a graveled path, Luvvy spied the low statue of a little curly headed girl on bended knee with her hands clasped together as if in prayer.

"Maudie!" exclaimed Luvvy. "That looks just like Maudie." She stared at the gravestone. "Poor little Lucy Beamer! She died when she was only six years old." She quickly put her hands to her face, and the violets dropped from her skirt to the grass.

"Don't cry, Luvvy," pleaded Agatha. "Somebody has already cried a lot for her, so it won't help."

Luvvy sniffled a few times, then stroked the statue's carved curls. "I'm going to leave the flowers here on her grave. She died so long ago that there's

probably nobody now to give her any."

They were less saddened by the monument to Barbara Fritchie, where a flag was flying from the plain shaft.

"After all, she was ninety-six years old when she died. And she still has a flag waving."

They chased a saucy chipmunk that led them to a rich bed of violets near the fence, and Luvvy replenished her supply.

It was finally time to go, and the nuns were having a task gathering all the girls together. The Big Girls were particularly hard to find. Luvvy even spied Betsey and Mary Leary hiding behind a big tombstone. The baskets were full of the little purple flowers, and those in the hands of the girls were beginning to wilt.

They left by a path that ran past a row of low headstones that were arranged in a single neat line. They belonged to Confederate soldiers, and many of them bore the single inscription, "Unknown."

"I think they're the saddest of all," said Luvvy. "I bet their families waited and prayed for them so long. Probably they waited and hoped for years after the war was over. It must be like that in Europe now. I'm glad President Wilson has kept us out of their war."

The walk back was tiresome now that the incentive of gathering violets was gone. The girls' steps lagged and the line straggled.

Agatha's steps lagged most. "I'm so tired," she said, "and I don't feel good."

"I shouldn't have taken you all past the Fritchie house," said Luvvy contritely. "Maybe that wore you out."

"No, I felt headachy during Mass this morning. And my throat is beginning to hurt."

"You must be catching a cold."

"I probably got it from Margaret Lane, that day pupil I sit with. She had a bad cold, and remember, she was absent Friday."

"I'll go with you to the infirmary to get something for it from Sister Mary Anne when we get back."

12.

Agatha

Sister Mary Anne made Agatha gargle for five minutes, and wrapped a woolen cloth around her throat. She advised her to be sure to wear her sweater when going outside.

"If you don't feel better by tomorrow, come back again," she ordered.

Agatha sat quietly in the big rocking chair in the playroom until supper. Luvvy kept her company although she would have liked to play outside with the other girls. They were playing one of her favorite games, London Bridge.

When the supper bell rang and they trooped into the refectory, Agatha seemed to revive at the sight of all the tables centered by low vases of violets.

"It looks like a party," she said.

"Like Commencement Week," added Mabel.

"That's not far off now," rejoiced Eunice.

But Luvvy noticed that Agatha hardly touched the creamed chipped beef, which she usually had second helpings of.

"I think I'll get permission to go on up to bed," she said after the meal. "My chest is beginning to hurt."

"You've been coughing too," said Luvvy anxiously, "and it sounds deep down. Mama says that's bad."

It was a lonely Sunday evening for Luvvy. She spent her time on her Monday lessons. She almost knew the history lesson word for word. Bedtime came as a relief. Agatha probably would feel better tomorrow. Luvvy fell asleep to the sound of Agatha's coughing in the next curtain.

When the girls lined up in the morning, Agatha wasn't among them. Her curtain was closed, too, but when Luvvy peeped into it, she was missing.

"The poor child was so sick during the night," explained Sister Mary Clotilde, the dormitory nun whose own curtain was near the door, "that I took her up to the infirmary. She has a bad cold in her chest."

Luvvy was disappointed, but she didn't worry too much. Betsey had been up there with a bad cold the time she had put wet blotters in her shoes. Luvvy counted the days she had been there. Four. She would face four days without Agatha.

She asked Sister Mary Clare if she might bring some books up to Agatha so she could keep up with her studies. It was really an excuse to see her.

Sister Mary Anne met her at the door and warned her not to get too close to the patient and not to stay too long.

Luvvy was surprised to see her best friend flat on her back with her eyes closed. Her cheeks were flushed, and when she opened her eyes, they were unusually bright. She looked much sicker than Betsey had.

"I'm so sorry, Agatha," she said. "I feel it's my fault for wearing you out on the trip to the cemetery."

"No—" Agatha began coughing so hard that she couldn't finish.

"You'll probably be up here for four days," said Luvvy, "but I'll come to see you often."

Agatha tried to speak, but coughed instead.

"You don't have to talk to me," said Luvvy. "I'll just talk to you." She tried to think of how she could carry on a monologue that wouldn't require any re-marks from the patient.

"I know what. Remember last fall we saw that man coming down in the parachute? No, don't answer. I know you remember."

Agatha nodded.

"I always wanted to write a story about it, and I've finally thought up a good one. It's about the war in Europe. There's a beautiful French girl named Nanette. She's a spy, and she's in love with a brave soldier named Pierre. Then the Huns capture her and imprison her in the attic of an old chateau. They're going to shoot her the next day. But Pierre jumps out of a flying machine and comes down with a parachute to rescue her."

Luvvy was inspired at seeing Agatha's eyes burning even more brightly.

"They try to escape but the Germans capture them in the courtyard. So they stand both of them against the wall before a firing squad. Just as they're ready to shoot, a company of French soldiers surround the chateau and rescue them."

Sister Mary Anne arrived at the door immediately after the rescue.

"Time is up, Luvena," she said. "You better leave now. I'm going to put another mustard plaster on Agatha's chest. The congestion should begin breaking up soon. You will probably find her much better tomorrow."

But next day, Luvvy wasn't even allowed to see her.

"She's worse," said Sister Mary Anne in a worried voice. "We expect the doctor almost any time now. We'll keep you posted on her condition."

It was a dreary afternoon. The Little Girls seemed to have lost any incentive for games during the recreation period.

They suddenly came to life at the harsh clanging of the emergency bell some days later. It was used for fires or other emergencies. They came running out, expecting to see smoke pouring from somewhere.

Girls were gathering on the grounds near the bread box window because Mother Mary Austin was standing there at the bell rope. Big Girls and Little Girls came running from doors and porches and stood in lines.

Mother Mary Austin waited until all seemed accounted for, then announced, "Girls, I have sad news for you. Little Agatha Mulcahy is seriously ill with pneumonia. I have gathered all of you together so that you may go to the chapel immediately and pray for her."

Luvvy felt as if one of the big trees had fallen on her. First Maudie and now Agatha. She knew that Reverend Mother never would have called them together this way if Agatha wasn't terribly sick.

Silently and soberly they marched up the porch stairs, through the hall, and into the chapel. They said their private prayers, and then Sister Veronica led them in the rosary. To Luvvy's dismay, now when she should have given her prayers complete attention, her mind kept wandering.

She remembered the prayers they had said for Maudie—and God hadn't answered them. And her memory of the cemetery outing was dismal. Some family must have prayed hard for little Lucy Beamer —and the "Unknowns"—and their prayers hadn't been answered. What good did it do to pray? But she went on mumbling the words anyway. She concentrated better when they said the Litany of the Blessed Virgin because the words were so beautiful. They made lovely pictures in one's mind. "Mystical rose . . . tower of ivory . . . house of gold . . ." But she felt ashamed that she wasn't able to pray with faith.

Next day more word of Agatha came by rumor. It wasn't known if she would live or die. She had a fifty-fifty chance. The doctor was coming twice a day.

Only Sister Veronica kept a smile on her face.

"She will recover," she assured Luvvy, "because we are all praying hard for her."

Luvvy was bursting to find out for herself how Agatha was getting along. Everything was rumor, rumor, rumor, and the nuns always tried to act so cheerful. Just like doctors. If she could only talk to Agatha herself. But now they had moved her into that room above the infirmary.

Hetty and Betsey were even worried about Luvvy for a few days, since she had been so close to Agatha.

A daring plan formed in Luvvy's mind. It came

during history class because she couldn't concentrate on the tariff question.

She raised her hand. "Sister, I have an awful headache. May I go up to the infirmary for some medicine or something?"

"Yes, dear," said Sister Mary Clare. "Perhaps you should lie down for awhile there. We wouldn't want you to get sick. And you and Agatha were together so much before she came down with pneumonia."

Luvvy hurried through halls and up stairs. But once she was near the infirmary door, she put her hand to her head and began to walk slowly.

"Sister," she told Sister Mary Anne, "I have an awful headache, and Sister Mary Clare told me I should lie down for awhile."

The infirmary nun began to cluck over Luvvy. She pulled back the coverlet of the bed and unlaced the girl's shoes.

"Now you just lie back and I'll put a cold pack on your forehead."

Sister wrung out a cloth in cold water.

"Oh, that feels good!" exclaimed Luvvy. "How is Agatha?"

"We hope for the best," said Sister, which was no answer to her question at all. "Now you just lie there quietly while I go down and see if there might be some ice in the kitchen."

Luvvy listened to her footsteps growing fainter in

the hall. Then she pushed aside the sodden cloth and jumped up. She went to a hot-air register by the stove, which was now cold, and sank to her knees.

"Agatha!" she called. "Can you hear me? Agatha!"

She put her ear against the grating. She seemed to hear a wheezing sound, then a hollow cough.

"Agatha, it's me!" She remembered composition and rhetoric. "It's I—Luvvy. How are you?"

There was a faint "All right." It didn't sound very convincing.

"You'll get well soon, won't you?"

A fainter "yes."

"Please try hard. You can do it if you try. You've got to get well because I've written to Mama that I want you to spend the summer with us. We'll have such fun. We'll go horseback riding and see Dixie and Nellie. You'll get well for that, won't you?"

She put her ear to the grating again, but all she heard was a rasping sound that might have been a chair scraping on the upper floor. It was followed by Sister Mary Anne's approaching footsteps.

Luvvy jumped up and quickly sat in a chair.

"I'm all right now, Sister," she said as the door opened. "That cold pack took care of my headache."

"Are you sure?" asked Sister Mary Anne. "It's a good thing, because the iceman hasn't come yet. And I must get back to Agatha."

"Oh, yes, I feel fine. May I go back to class

now? I hate to miss out on anything."

On the way down the stairs, she passed the chapel door. She decided to go inside and say another prayer. Now there would be nothing to distract her. She would have God's ear all to herself. It must be distracting to Him to have so many prayers coming at the same time—like everybody in the class asking Sister Mary Clare something all at once.

In the empty chapel with the red sanctuary light flickering, she felt so much closer to God. First she said a perfunctory Our Father and Hail Mary. Then she spoke directly to Him. She began to bargain.

"If you'll let Agatha get well, I'll never whisper or giggle in church again. I'll keep my mind on my prayers, and I'll try to obey the Sisters in everything. Please! Please!"

She sought more help to convince Him. She called upon Maudie.

"You're up there now, Maudie. Remember the time you said that if I'd take you for a walk to Pansy's house you'd do something for me? And I didn't think there was anything a little girl like you could do for me? But I took you anyhow. You used to get most anything you wanted because you nagged so. I want you to do something for me now. Please keep nagging Him to make Agatha well."

When Luvvy rose from her knees, she was filled with peace and hope. Agatha would get well. Maudie

would see to it. Why hadn't she thought of her before?

So when she heard the emergency bell ring next morning, she was stricken with sharp despair. They were going to be told that Agatha had died. She remembered when she first had suspected that Maudie was dead. How she had run away to the attic so no one could actually tell her. She had that same feeling of panic now. She wanted to run into the coat room, bolt the door and pull one of the coats over her head.

But she slowly walked into formation with the other girls. She stood with bowed head so she could not see Mother Mary Austin's face.

There was a silence, then she heard Reverend Mother's voice.

"Girls, I couldn't wait to tell all of you the happy news that little Agatha Mulcahy will live. She passed the crisis last night, and is now on the road to recovery. So you may go to the chapel immediately and say a prayer of thanksgiving."

Luvvy began weeping as hard as if the news had actually been of her death. All the worry and unhappiness and tension of the past few days flowed away in tears.

She ran to tell Sister Veronica how happy she was at the news. Sister seemed surprised.

"But we knew she would get well," she said, "because we said so many prayers for her."

13.

"The Arab's Farewell to His Steed"

Commencement Week didn't turn out to be the gay week-long festival that Luvvy had imagined from the Girls' stories.

"But I told you we had to do a lot of practicing for Commencement Day," Hetty reminded her.

"You didn't say we'd have to practice marching into the music room and up on the stage, morning, noon, and night," complained Luvvy. "I'm sick of practicing."

She was thrilled when Miss Font le Roy informed her, "I have chosen you to recite 'The Arab's Farewell to His Steed' on the program, Luvena, because you do it so dramatically."

Ah, the glory of it! She remembered how proud the family had been because Betsey had recited "Lord Ullin's Daughter" the year before. But, oh the pain! She had to recite it over and over for Miss Font le Roy's critical appraisal. And she would have to stand up before a room full of people of all ages.

Despite rigid rehearsals, the nuns became more lenient in other ways. Girls walked on the grass and ran in the halls without rebuke.

Some of them went arm in arm openly chanting:

> *A few more days and I'll be free*
> *From this house of misery,*

Or

> *No more biscuits, no more buns,*
> *No more fighting with convent nuns.*

The nuns who heard only smiled amiably.

Agatha chanted the little ditties loudest because she would be leaving the convent for a whole summer with Luvvy's family. She had fully recovered from her illness by now, and had even put on a few extra pounds.

"I'm sick of all this rehearsing too," she admitted to the other Little Girls.

"Now, Agatha," admonished Amy, "you wouldn't want to shame all of us by falling on the steps or sitting in the wrong chair and mixing up the line."

Somehow, Amy's holier-than-thou ways didn't irritate Luvvy anymore.

"I really hate to leave the girls for a whole summer," she confessed to Betsey. "I'll even miss Amy. She's one of us."

"There has to be an Amy in every convent school to make it complete," reasoned Betsey.

The morning of Commencement Day filled the convent grounds and rooms with an unfamiliar assortment of people. Parents and grandparents, uncles and aunts, older and younger brothers and sisters. A gaggling bunch of Old Girls, as former students were called, always returned as faithfully as migrating birds to their nesting place.

And there was Amy's mother, blazing with diamonds, and Mabel's father and little sisters who shared her red hair.

Most important of all were Papa and Mama. They had only come for the day, and therefore were not staying at Mrs. Young's boarding house as they sometimes did. Regina had generously offered to remain home with the baby and Marylou so they could go.

All the pupils wore white dresses. Agatha's was the prettiest of all—a lace guimpe and a waterfall of ruffles—because the nuns had made it for her with their own hands. No hand-me-down, that.

It was a solemn moment when all the guests were seated in the big music room and the girls nervously lined up outside. The triumphant notes of "Pomp and Circumstance" showered from the piano and fell on the ears of the waiting girls. The lines began marching in. No one fell on the stairs or sat in the wrong chair. How could they after all that practice? The graduating class, including Hetty, sat on the stage.

It was a long, long program that began with harp and piano solos and duets. Luvvy grew more nervous as it moved along. She wished she had never been chosen to give the recitation. Suppose she fainted on the stage! Her skirt might even fly up above her knees —the shame of it! She would be remembered not only as the girl who had hung by her knees from the porch, but as the girl who fainted on the stage at Commencement and exposed her drawers.

Miss Font le Roy took the center of the stage. She looked more stylish than ever in her white linen suit.

"Next we will have a recitation, by Luvena Marie Savage, of 'The Arab's Farewell to His Steed,' " she announced in pear-shaped tones.

Luvena Marie was stricken by stage fright. It was as if she had heard, "Next to mount the scaffold and put her head on the block will be hapless Luvena Savage."

How could she ever get up before this enormous audience to recite her piece? Her mouth was dry. Her throat was tight. Her hands were clammy. She wished she could be somebody in the audience who would only have to listen.

"Good luck!" whispered Agatha, squeezing her hand. "You can do it." Agatha instinctively knew just how she felt.

Luvvy climbed the steps and faced the audience as bravely as Mary, Queen of Scots. The sea of faces made her dizzy. Then she saw Papa and Mama's proud faces among them. She couldn't shame them on this happy day.

She began in a tremulous voice:

> My beautiful! My beautiful that standeth
>   meekly by,
> With thy proudly-arched and glossy neck, and
>   dark and fiery eye.

The faces of the audience began to disintegrate. They spread into a waste of sandy desert. She was alone with Pepper, the dead horse she had loved so. All the grief and loss she had felt when she heard about his fatal accident went into her voice.

> The morning sun shall dawn again, but never
>   more with thee
> Shall I gallop o'er the desert paths, where we
>   were wont to be.

Never again would she offer Pepper sugar lumps

or stand on his broad back. She felt the sorrow and despair of the Arab who had sold his devoted horse.

> Slow and unmounted shall I roam, with weary step alone,
> Where with fleet step and joyous bound thou oft hast borne me on.

The big room had become as silent as a church.

In some places she could hardly go on, but it wasn't because of stage fright. She could still ride Valley and Dolly but never again Pepper. Sobs broke into her words.

She could scarcely wait to get to the joyful ending. She wished it could have ended that way with her circus horse.

> Who said that I had given thee up? Who said that thou wert sold?
> 'Tis false!—'tis false! my Arab steed! I fling them back their gold.

Luvvy made such a violent gesture of flinging the gold that a Very Little Girl in the front row ducked.

The recitation was over. Luvvy wiped her eyes and walked off the stage to thunderous applause. She had a brief glimpse of Miss Font le Roy's beaming face.

The emotions of the audience were calmed by another piano solo. Then the real business of the day got underway.

The valedictory was given by one of Hetty's friends. Many corrections and suggestions from Sister Mary Pauline, and coaching by Miss Font le Roy had shaped it. Luvvy was hypnotized by the eloquence.

"Our convent training has woven golden threads into the shimmering fabric of our characters. The warp is the sound scholarly knowledge we have imbibed, the woof the strong thread of spiritual values inculcated by our devoted teachers."

Beautiful composition and rhetoric, and correct Delsarte breathing, ended with "So now we graduates have the courage to embark upon the sea of life, with its vicissitudes and temptations, in a strong galleon of wisdom, piety, and resolution."

Luvvy tried to imagine the bevy of young girls in long white dresses sailing down the Potomac on an iron-plated *Monitor* to do battle with the enemy.

After endless speeches, there was the presentation of awards by Father Kane, the pastor of St. John's. They went from gold medals for scholarship, deportment, and other achievements, to books for lesser accomplishments.

As Luvvy had expected, "The gold medal for deportment in the lower grades is awarded to Amy Ackroyd for the virtuous example of piety and obedience she has given to the other girls."

When they reached the distribution of books, Luvvy was pleased to have her name called. She mounted the stage again, curtsied to Father Kane, and received a book.

She returned to her chair slowly as she had practiced. "Do not race back to your seat as if the stage has suddenly caught fire," Miss Font le Roy had impressed upon them.

Not until she was safely seated again did she dare look at the title of the book. Her eyes fell upon the familiar gilded letters circled by flowers. It was *Agnes of the Lilies.*

As she opened to the fly page, Agatha and Mabel leaned over her shoulders to look. In peerless Palmer handwriting was the inscription, "To Luvena Marie Savage for excellence in composition and rhetoric." Lightly written at the bottom of the page was "For a budding author from her appreciative teacher" with Sister Mary Clare's signature.

Luvvy's dislike for little Agnes was exorcised at last. She felt a gentle tolerance for the saintly child. All girls were different, and you had to accept them as they were if you wanted friends.

She was glad that Amy had won the gold deportment medal. She was glad that her recitation was over. She was glad that Mama and Papa were so close. She was happiest that after this long-drawn-out program was over, they would all climb into the Machine and go home for the summer. A whole lazy, happy summer with Agatha. Even when the summer was over, she and Agatha would be returning to the Visitation Academy together. They would be Big Girls then.

Format by Phoebe Amsterdam
Set in 12 pt. Kenntonian
Composed by Haddon Craftsmen, Inc.
Printed by Murray Printing Co.
Bound by American Book Stratford Press
HARPER & ROW, PUBLISHERS, INC.

71 72 73 74   12 11 10 9 8 7 6 5 4 3 2 1